SOUL SENT[_]
SET AND

CW01521747

Becca Van

MENAGE EVERLASTING

Siren Publishing, Inc.
www.SirenPublishing.com

A SIREN PUBLISHING BOOK
IMPRINT: Ménage Everlasting

SOUL SENTINELS 1: SET AND SAB
Copyright © 2016 by Becca Van

ISBN: 978-1-68295-235-1

First Printing: June 2016

Cover design by Les Byerley
All art and logo copyright © 2016 by Siren Publishing, Inc.

Printed in the U.S.A.

PUBLISHER
Siren Publishing, Inc.
www.SirenPublishing.com

DEDICATION

Just a quick note to tell you how I came about this series. I actually had a nightmare and dreamt that someone or something was tugging at my chest, trying to rip my soul out of my body. Needless to say it took me a long time to get back to sleep.

It's amazing what our brains can envisage even when we are asleep.

A couple of days later I remembered the dream and the premise for this series was born.

Also a big thanks to Pat for the hard work done in editing the story. I really appreciate your suggestions and help.

I would like to dedicate this book to all my loyal readers. If it wasn't for you all I wouldn't be where I am today. Thank you from the bottom of my heart.

Wishing you all the best in the festive season. Stay safe and Happy New Year.

Love Becca. xxoo

SOUL SENTINELS 1:
SET AND SAB

BECCA VAN

Prologue

Setau tilted his head as he stood beneath the clear glass dome in the Temple of Ra. He basked in the warmth of the sun warming and caressing over his skin. The sun's rays filled him with power and vitality, cleansing away the tiredness that seemed to plague his very soul of late.

He and the other sentinels had spent century upon century protecting the humans against the evil ones and although he loved doing the sun god's bidding, he felt so alone. He loved the other sentinels as if they were of his own blood but he couldn't help feeling that something was missing.

He'd watched human beings forge ahead from being little more than intelligent apes to what they were today and even though he sometimes resented those he and his comrades protected, he couldn't help what he was feeling. Resentful over the fact that the ones they saved had the choice of finding love and creating a family. He and the other sentinels had spent millennia alone and he craved having a woman he could love, hold and cherish.

Set knew he should be content with his lot since no other species he knew of beside their enemy's leader was immortal, but he was restless and no matter what he did, he couldn't seem to settle.

"What troubles you, my son?" Ra's booming voice echoed through the temple, making him start. The sun god had only ever come to him and the others in their dreams or when they were grievously wounded, which thankfully so far hadn't necessitated in Ra coming to his or the others' aid. He and the others had had wounds that had weakened them, but they'd circumvented that problem by taking blood from a human or two. They were always careful to not take too much and had the ability to wipe the experience from the human's mind.

"I…don't know, my lord," Setau answered, not really sure how to explain what he was feeling.

"Stand," Ra ordered.

Set took a deep breath and rose to his feet. When he opened his eyes he was stunned to see the sun god standing before him. He quickly lowered his head in deference to his deity, hoping he had not blundered by looking at the god.

"You have all served me well and for such a long time. I am very proud to call you my sentinels."

"Thank you, my lord."

"It is I who should be thanking you all. If not for you and your men, the demonic would have obliterated the humans centuries past."

Set didn't know what to say to that, so he remained quiet. Ra was right, though. If it hadn't been for him and the others the demons would have killed off all of mankind long ago. They were an evil race that survived by ripping souls from bodies and feeding off their essence. The demonic were only able to solidify from shadow form after consuming human spirits but he and his comrades had put a stop to that. In fact, for the last thirty years the demonic had been quiet but Set had a feeling that the peace wouldn't last.

"You shall all be rewarded for your loyalty and diligence in keeping the humans safe." Ra's booming voice pulled him from his thoughts and back to the present.

"My lord?"

Ra moved close to Set and although he was tempted to see his deity face to face, it just wasn't done. To see the sun god in a dream wasn't the same as being in his actual presence. And that was something that puzzled him, too. Other than the one and only time Ra had chosen him and the other sentinels, he had never met him or the other immortals face to face.

"Look at me, Setau Abasi," Ra ordered.

Set obeyed the command, and his gaze met the sun god's pure golden eyes.

"The time of peace is over. Apep is gathering his shadow followers and from what I have gathered there are many. The humans are once more in danger."

"We will seek them out, my lord."

Ra placed his hand on Set's shoulder. Power and peace surged through his body but that wasn't all. He felt a tingling heat on his left pectoral and although he was tempted to look away from his deity, he refrained. When he felt the same tingling at his left shoulder blade he wanted to ask what was happening, but he waited patiently, knowing his god would explain things in his own good time. To question a divinity wouldn't be conducive to good health. Ra was known infamously for his temper and the last thing Set wanted to do was invoke the god's rage.

"I know you will. Come back to my temple tomorrow at high noon but bring the other sentinels with you."

"Your will, will be done, my lord." Set bowed his head as Ra removed his hand from his shoulder and backed away. He knew the moment Ra was gone. The power and peace which had been coursing through his veins waned. The restlessness and loneliness returned. It didn't seem to matter that he had the companionship of seven other sentinels, nor that they were as close, if not closer, than brothers of blood. He'd been plagued with restiveness for the last three decades and no matter what he did, the feeling just grew stronger. Ra had said that the peace was over. Maybe a good fight would help take the edginess away.

If Apep was up to his old tricks then he and the others were going to be busy. Apep was a snake god, and had and did use the souls of evil beings to do his bidding. If Apep had been amassing more malevolent spirits over the last thirty years, Set knew that they were going to be busy each and every night hunting those demonic shadows down and trying to keep the humans safe.

Set drew in a deep breath and lifted his face to the sun once more. He and his comrades would need to get as much rest as they could before the fighting began. Their nights were going to be endless, but that's what Ra had recruited them for.

He glanced down at his chest, his breath hitching in his throat when he saw the mark of Ra on his left pectoral muscle. The eye of Ra was only ever given to those the god honored. He was amazed that his deity would do such after millennia but who was he to question him. The mark looked like it had been tattooed into his skin and yet other than a slight warmth he'd felt no pain. Ra must have made sure of that. Although after all the centuries of battling the demonic, Set and the others were used to pain.

Set walked toward the large kitchen but paused outside the door to the small suite he shared with Sabu. After seeing Ra's mark on his chest he remembered a tingling feeling on his back, too, and was curious. It wouldn't matter if he delayed relaying Ra's words to the other sentinels for a few moments. He pushed open the door and stalked toward the en-suite bathroom off his bedroom and turned his back toward the mirror. He gasped when he saw the outline of a falcon on his left shoulder blade. It wasn't overly big but it wasn't small either. The outline was black but the feathers were brown and the detail was amazing, but what caught his eye were the falcon's eyes. They were the same golden color as Ra's astonishing orbs. Set had no idea what the marks signified other than to show that he was one of Ra's sentinels. He would have to remember to ask his god tomorrow and whether the other sentinels would also receive the marks, but for now he needed to inform the others of the coming war.

He just hoped that this war with the demonic didn't last for hundreds of years like the previous one had. Set was getting tired of fighting all the time. He wished the peace had lasted longer and although he'd been bored, he'd liked not having to fight. That didn't mean he and the others didn't continue to train, because they did each and every day. Honing their skills with the blessed blades Ra had bestowed upon them was a necessity when they had been appointed as Soul Sentinels to the humans. It was their job to make sure the humans didn't have their spirits ripped from their bodies by the demonic shadows and would continue to be so as long as humans were alive. Since the human population had exploded into the billions, he didn't see their job coming to an end anytime soon.

Chapter One

Zara bolted upright, covered in sweat and feeling so scared her heart felt like it was about to pound right out through her chest. Night after night she'd had weird nightmares. No matter what she did before bed to tire herself out, nothing stopped the nightmare from coming. First she'd tried running on the treadmill until she was ready to drop and then she'd lifted weights. Even drinking wine hadn't been enough to send her into oblivion so she could sleep through the night.

She had no idea what the dreams meant or why they plagued her but she was fed up. Fed up with the arrogant prick she worked for, fed up with being alone, and fed up from the broken sleep.

She'd been working for Jim Connell for the last five years and she'd had to convince herself nearly every day that the money was worth the grief, but she wasn't so sure of that anymore. It was getting harder and harder to hold her tongue and not give her boss the tongue lashing he so richly deserved. Jim should have been born in the eighteenth or nineteenth century when women were nothing better than chattel.

Resigned to the fact she wasn't about to get any more sleep, she tossed the covers aside and headed for the kitchen. After getting a glass of water and sitting on a stool at the counter, she tried to figure out why she was having such weird dreams.

The nightmare was the same each and every night and although it didn't last more than a few seconds, she always woke up terrified, with her heart racing and her body covered in sweat. Zara had no idea what it meant and wished she could find out, if the dream did in fact mean something.

She would be deeply asleep only to surface to feel as if someone or something was trying to rip her soul out of her body. She always woke before whoever or whatever succeeded, thank goodness, and although the tugging was painful but not to the point of agony, it was also a scary feeling.

Zara rolled the cool glass of water over her forehead and sighed. She dreaded going to sleep each night and when she did manage to drift off, she awoke after only a few hours of shut-eye. She was weary to the bone and didn't know how much longer she could go on like this, but nothing she did alleviated her hope of remaining in a deep dreamless sleep. Maybe working for her asshole of a boss and the stress she dealt with each day while dealing with him was manifesting into that horrible dream. And if that was the case then she needed to leave. As that thought crossed her mind, the confidence in her decision grew and she knew it was the right choice to make. Tomorrow first thing she was going to hand in her resignation notice. She had a little bit of money put aside and she could last a couple of weeks on that while she searched for another job.

Decision made, Zara drained the water from her glass and headed back to bed, hoping to get a couple more hours of sleep in before her alarm went off.

* * * *

Zara gritted her teeth when Jim demanded the insurance file on a client. She wasn't pissed about doing something for him. It was his tone that got her dander up. Her boss was an out and out asshole. When she handed him the file he requested he didn't even say thank you. She hurried back to her desk and quickly typed her resignation, read it over and took a deep breath before hitting the send button.

She was just pondering how long he would take before he acknowledged her email but it wasn't as long as she expected. He must have seen the subject heading when the email hit his in box.

"Zara, get your ass in here. Now!" Jim bellowed.

She drew in another deep breath and released it before rising from her chair. Feeling a little more fortified, she pushed her shoulders back and kept her head high as she entered his office.

"What the fuck, Zara? You can't do this. I took you on straight out of college and this is how you repay me! You ungrateful little bitch." Jim's face was red and the veins in his neck and forehead stood out from beneath his skin. He looked like he was ready to explode and she knew that nothing she said would get through to him and she wasn't up to dealing with his shit. She was tired and had a headache the size of Mt. Vesuvius. She didn't have the energy to deal with him so she decided it would be prudent to leave right now.

"Thanks for the opportunity but I can't work for you anymore. Make sure you put my last paycheck and holiday pay into my bank account. Good luck finding someone else to put up with your arrogant angry ass." Zara spun on her heel, grabbed her purse from the drawer in her desk, and walked out the door into the spring air and sunshine. She hadn't meant to say any of those things to Jim but her tongue had gotten away with her. As she walked across the main street of her hometown of Price, Utah, she could still hear Jim screaming obscenities. However, Zara felt as if a huge weight had been shifted from her shoulders and knew she'd made the right choice.

She walked into the diner and took a seat.

"How you doing, honey?" Mathilda, the middle aged owner and waitress, greeted her.

"Great," Zara answered with a smile.

"You're kind of early for lunch, aren't you?" Mathilda asked after glancing at the clock on the wall above the kitchen doorway.

"Yes. I quit."

"You did?" Mathilda's mouth dropped open before she smiled. "Good for you, honey. I don't know how you worked for him as long as you did. Jim's an ass."

"Yes he is," Zara agreed.

"So what'll you have?"

"Are you still serving breakfast? I didn't get time to eat this morning."

"Yeah."

"Okay, I'll have a bacon and egg toasted sandwich and coffee."

"Coming right up." Mathilda poured her coffee from a freshly brewed pot and then took her order to the kitchen.

When the bell over the door tinkled softly Zara looked up and toward the door. Her heart flipped and she gasped when she saw eight very tall, handsome muscular men enter. She looked at each of them, trying to be surreptitious and not too obvious but when her gaze snagged on the last two men, she squirmed in her seat. Her nipples hardened and her clit throbbed. Her pussy clenched and juices dripped onto her panties.

Zara had seen handsome men before but had never reacted like this. She didn't understand why her body was so responsive to two complete strangers, but she couldn't deny the lust running rampant in her veins as she looked at them.

They sat in two separate booths and she understood why when four of them filled the space with their wide shoulders and muscular bodies. They were all wearing black. Black leather pants and jeans, T-shirts and leather jackets. She wondered if they were a motorcycle gang but when she looked out the window she didn't see any motorbikes, but they could have parked down the street and then walked to the diner. She didn't know if they were residents of Price but didn't think so since she'd never seen them before. However, she didn't know everyone in town so they might live here.

Mathilda came out from the back, grabbed the coffee pot, and poured some of the dark brew for the eight men. "What can I get you all?"

Zara didn't take any notice of what the men ordered because she was too enthralled by their deep voices and handsome faces, and although she tried to keep her eyes to herself she found them on those two men again, and again.

One had black hair that was tied up at his nape and since it wasn't a long ponytail she imagined that it would fall around his shoulders when down. His eyes were a startling bright green color and although he wasn't handsome in the classic model way, he was appealing to look at. He had a rugged countenance she couldn't ignore, with a long slightly crooked nose which she figured had been broken at some time in his life. His cheekbones were sharp and his jaw strong. There was a slight dusting of stubble on his jaw, as if he hadn't taken the time to shave that morning. She had to draw her gaze away from him when the urge to reach out and touch him almost got the better of her.

Her gaze moved to the man next to him and although he wasn't looking at her, she felt as if he and his friend were aware of her perusal. This guy had short dark brown hair and his eyes were a light blue color. His cheekbones weren't as sharp but he was no less handsome than the other man. Her breath caught in her throat when he smiled. He had two small dimples at each side of his lips that gave the impression that he could be sweet, maybe even harmless. However, Zara had a feeling that was far from the truth. They all had an aura of power but these two men seemed to get her libido revving more so than the other six. Zara had never been turned on by dominance or authority before but on those two men that confident visage just seemed to get her right in the core.

"Here ya go, honey," Mathilda said as she placed a plate in front of Zara. "Enjoy."

"Thanks." Zara picked up her knife and fork and began to eat. When the food hit her tongue it tasted bland and she put it down to nervousness at having so many handsome men so close but she continued to eat and tried to ignore them as best she could.

"Miss? Excuse me, miss. Can we please borrow your salt shaker?"

Zara turned her head and looked up and up and up. When her eyes met those green ones she stopped breathing. It took her a couple of seconds to realize she was staring but thankfully her mouth wasn't gaping open. "What?"

"Can we please borrow your salt?"

"Uh, yeah. Sorry." Zara grabbed the salt shaker and handed it to him. The moment his fingers brushed hers as he took the small bottle from her, heat singed her flesh and shot straight down to her pussy. It took everything she had not to moan. When she noticed her hand was still hovering in the air she quickly lowered it and her head, trying to hide her face as heat suffused her cheeks. She glanced at him from the corner of her eye and was surprised to see him still standing beside her, staring at her.

"Thank you." His baritone voice was smooth and sent shivers racing up and down her spine but since she was having difficulty finding a reply she nodded instead. She sighed softly in relief and resignation when he walked back to his own seat and it was only then she realized that seven other pairs of eyes were fixed on her.

One of the men spoke in a voice so quiet she couldn't hear his words but she was glad because they all turned from her and began talking amongst themselves. The tension in her muscles eased and she was able to breathe a little easier.

Zara finished eating and sipped on the coffee Mathilda had refilled in her cup and she was trying to figure out what she was going to do now that she was unemployed. She reached into her purse for her smart phone and began surfing the net for jobs in the local area, but when she didn't find anything a sigh of frustration escaped.

"Are you all right, hon?" Mathilda asked as she sat across from Zara.

"Yes, just trying to figure out what to do next."

Mathilda made a noise in the back of her throat. "You look exhausted, Zara. What have you been doing to yourself?"

"I'm having trouble sleeping." Zara glanced to the side from beneath her lashes and although the men didn't seem to be paying her any attention she had a feeling the two closest to her across the way had her undivided attention. She gave a mental shrug and decided she was imagining things because of her weariness.

"That's not a surprise since you were working for that idiot."

Zara shook her head. "I've been having nightmares. The same one every night for the past month. No matter what I do to tire myself out I always end up waking with my heart pounding in my chest and covered in sweat."

"What's the dream about?" Mathilda asked.

"It's weird."

Mathilda waved her hand in the air and made a "pfft" sound. "Aren't all dreams and nightmares? Tell me."

Zara found herself telling Mathilda about her strange recurring dream and when she'd finished she waited for the older woman to tell her she was nuts.

"It's probably stress from having to deal with Jim every day. Now that you've quit you can relax. Stress can do some pretty awful things to a body. You mark my words, girl, you'll probably sleep like a baby tonight."

"I hope so, Mathilda. I don't think I can go on like this much longer."

Mathilda nodded and patted her hand. "Maybe you should go on home and have a nap."

"I'm not sure it will work. I've never been able to sleep in the middle of the day."

* * * *

Setau met Sabu's gaze when he heard the young beautiful woman retell her dream to the waitress. His body tensed and he went on full alert. After meeting in Ra's Temple beneath the Utah lake near Provo, their deity had explained about the growing activity of the demonic in the underworld, and he'd also given the rest of the sentinels the marks of Ra on their chests and backs.

When he heard the woman explain about her concurrent nightmare, he was very concerned. It seemed the shadows weren't yet strong enough to steal the spirits from the living but Set had no doubt it wouldn't be long before they succeeded. It was up to them to find the shadows and destroy them before their power grew, but the only way to do that was lie in wait as evil tried to rip souls from humans. How was he supposed to explain to the woman sitting in the booth across from theirs that she was in danger, being hunted by evil? And if she did believe him, would she agree to come back to their hideout so they could protect her?

"What are we going to do?" Sabu asked.

Set shrugged. "I don't know." He looked to his friends and they all shook their heads. Set knew that although they had continued talking quietly, the others had been aware of every word the woman told the waitress. Because they were demigods as well as warriors they all had exceptional hearing, smell, and eyesight. They were also very strong and fast. He and the other sentinels could move faster than the human eye could see, which came in handy when they had previously fought the demonic.

He took a deep breath and when the scent of aroused woman reached his nose, he shifted in his seat. His cock had been half hard from the moment he'd set eyes on her when he had entered the diner, but now it was at full mast. His skin itched as if something had crawled beneath it but he refrained from scratching and drawing attention to himself. Sabu moved in his seat, drawing his gaze and from the way the man had his teeth clenched and he couldn't seem to get comfortable he realized that his best friend was also fighting his attraction to the beautiful young woman.

The words Ra had spoken two days previously echoed in his mind. *"You shall all be rewarded for your loyalty and diligence in keeping the humans safe."* Set had no idea why he was suddenly thinking of that so he pushed those thoughts from his mind. What he should be doing was planning with his men but this time and place wasn't exactly appropriate. And he couldn't seem to keep his mind or his gaze from the gorgeous blonde still chatting with the waitress. His muscles were pumped and his cock was hard. There was something about her that drew her to him and he didn't want to let her leave his sight.

"Damn it! She's leaving," Sabu murmured. "What are we going to do?"

"I think we need to follow her," Pentu whispered.

"I agree." Paser nodded.

"From what we heard about her dreams, she's a demonic target." Nehi drained the coffee from his cup and shoved his empty plate away.

"It's our job to protect the innocent," Menna mumbled. "And I have to tell you that I wouldn't mind in the least protecting that sexy little body."

Setau's hackles rose and before he knew he was going to, he was growling low in his throat. Sabu's low rumble joined his.

"What's with you two?" Mitry asked with a frown.

"I think they have the hots for her." Weni smirked and waggled his eyebrows.

Setau ignored his comrades' teasing, dropped enough money on the table to cover their bill and a generous tip, and strode toward the door. He glanced about and sighed with relief when he saw the woman walking along the street and it just so happened she was moving toward where they had parked their bikes.

"What are we going to do, Set?" Sabu asked as they followed.

"The only thing we can do is tell her the truth."

"And if she thinks we're crazy?" Sab asked.

Set shrugged. In all the centuries he'd been alive he'd never even considered telling a human about who and what they were or about the demonic. The woman was probably going to laugh in his face and then run in fear.

He watched the gentle sway of her hips and if it were at all possible his cock hardened even more and his gums itched as if his fangs were about to descend. That hadn't happened to him since he'd first been changed. He'd learned to control his body's urges but something about this woman had him acting like a randy teenager.

"I want her, Set." The possessiveness in Sab's voice echoed what he was feeling.

"I do, too."

"Do you think Ra has decided we've been alone long enough?"

Set nearly stumbled and he glanced at Sab again.

"Do you think he's finally decided we're worthy of having a mate?"

Set stopped and once more Ra's words about being rewarded echoed in his mind. Was this what he'd meant? Had he sent this woman to him and Sab?

If that was the case then they needed to talk her into coming back to their underground home. The thought of her being targeted by the demonic sent rage coursing through his veins and his heart flipped.

He knew that Ra had no control over Apep or his shadow minions but if this woman was their mate, then why was she being targeted now? Did Apep somehow know she was meant to be theirs? Set couldn't work out how the underworld leader could possibly know such a thing when he hadn't even known himself.

One thing was certain, though.

He would give his immortal soul to keep her safe.

Chapter Two

Zara knew she was being followed. She'd heard the bell over the entrance to the diner tinkle as she walked down the street. Her heart began to race and her muscles tensed in preparation to flee, but when she got to the corner and looked right she nearly sagged with relief. Eight big black motorcycles gleamed in the sunlight and she realized that the men weren't following her but heading toward their vehicles.

Her heart slowed and the tension eased. She was so relieved she closed her eyes for a second or two and the next thing she knew she was falling toward the concrete. A startled cry left her lips and she put her arm out to try and lessen the impact. Another pain-filled cry left her mouth when she heard and felt a sickening crack, her arm buckling under her weight, as she fell chest down onto the hard ground. She wanted to move but she was in agony. Her wrist was hurting so bad she felt sick to her stomach. She had no idea what she'd tripped over, but right now she wished she could go back in time a couple of seconds. If she could she wouldn't have closed her damn eyes, and maybe she wouldn't be in so much pain.

"Are you all right?"

Zara glanced through tear blurry eyes to the man she'd seen in the diner. She wanted to answer him but she was scared if she opened her mouth she would scream with pain, so she shook her head.

"Fuck! It looks like her wrist is broken." Another man she'd seen in the diner squatted near her head.

"I'm going to pick you up, but I'll be careful. Okay?"

Zara nodded. If they didn't help her up from the ground she just might end up lying there all day long.

"Guide her hurt arm close to her body."

Zara closed her eyes when large warm hands landed on her shoulders and another gripped the elbow of her right arm. She drew in a deep breath and held it. She was glad she did when the two men helped her into a sitting position. A whimper escaped when the man holding her elbow gently guided her arm toward her chest.

"Sorry."

Zara nodded again.

"Is she okay?"

"We need to get her to a hospital. I'm Setau and the man in front of you is Sabu. I'll introduce the others to you later."

"Zara," she managed to croak out.

"Okay, Zara, we're going to get you on your feet," Setau said. "Are you ready?"

Zara drew in another deep breath and nodded.

"Okay, here we go."

She clenched her jaw to stop another whimper from escaping her mouth as the two men helped her to her feet. She swayed and perspiration broke out on her brow and upper lip.

"Do you have a car we can drive you to the hospital in?" Sabu asked.

If she hadn't been in excruciating pain she would have shivered at the deep gravelly cadence of his voice. She couldn't believe her body was reacting to Setau's and Sabu's close proximity and their sexy voices.

"No," she whispered her answer.

"We could call the paramedics?" Setau suggested.

"No. I'll get a taxi."

"You don't think we're going to leave you when you're hurt, do you?" Setau asked.

"I'll be fine."

"Sure you will," Sabu replied sarcastically.

"I'll take her on the bike," Setau said. "Get her purse, Pen."

"I don't think…"

"Shh, you'll be safe. I'll be careful," Setau said.

Zara wasn't about to stand here arguing because she was feeling worse and in more pain with each passing second. She shifted on her feet and closed her eyes when she wavered.

"Hold her arm secure," Setau ordered and then she was being swept up into his arms.

She rested her head on his chest and breathed in and out through her nose and mouth to try and circumvent the nausea roiling in her belly.

"Start the bike for me." The low rumble of his voice against her ear was comforting and she relaxed into his hold.

"Okay, baby, you ready?" Setau asked.

Zara nodded once more.

"Hold that arm tight against your chest. I'll try not to jostle you too much."

She felt Setau move and then she was being lowered onto his hard thighs crossways. His arms reached for the handlebars on his bike, caging her in.

"Don't worry about falling off. I won't let you. You just worry about keeping that arm still. Okay?"

Tears leaked from behind her closed eyelids but she managed to answer. "Thank you."

"You're welcome, baby."

"Here, put the helmet on her," Sab said. "Sit her up a bit, and I'll put it on for her."

Zara drew another deep breath and with Set's help sat up a bit straighter. Sab gently pushed the helmet down over her head and then secured the straps. The whole time he worked, she stared into his amazing blue eyes. When he was done, he gave her a wink and turned toward his own bike. She slumped against Set's chest and squeezed her lids closed.

Zara wanted to open her eyes and take in the sights from the motorbike when they began to move, but she was too intent on not breaking down and blubbering like an idiot. She could hear the rumbles of the other bikes as they followed and although it seemed to take them hours to reach the hospital, she knew it was only minutes.

The bike stopped, and Set removed the helmet from her head before passing it off to someone behind her. Before she could blink, Setau lifted her back into his arms and began walking. The sterile smell of disinfectant assailed her nose and she knew they were inside the hospital.

"I'm Doctor Gillette. What's happened?"

"She fell over. We think her wrist is broken," Setau answered.

"I need a gurney," the doctor yelled.

"I can carry her," Setau said. "The faster we get to where we're going the quicker you can give her a shot for the pain."

"Are you family?" Doctor Gillette asked.

"I'm her fiancé."

Zara couldn't believe he'd just said that but knew the doctor would boot him out if he wasn't someone close to her. Although she was in a great deal of pain she was comfortable in his arms and didn't want him to leave. Which was completely crazy since she didn't even know the man.

"Place her on the table. I need to get an X-ray," the doctor ordered.

Zara opened her eyes and stared at the big man as he backed away to allow the doctor to examine her. He gently gripped her elbow and pulled her arm away from her body. She clamped her teeth together so hard she wondered if she would break one. When tears formed in her eyes again she squeezed her lids shut but it didn't stop the moisture from trickling down her cheeks.

"You're hurting her," Setau said angrily.

"I need to see how much damage there is."

"You need to give her some pain relief first," Setau demanded.

"I was about to," the doctor answered. "If you can't let me do my job then you should leave."

Zara heard Setau growl. "I'm not going anywhere."

She looked toward the door when it opened and met Sabu's gaze. "What's going on?"

Sabu and Setau both looked angry enough to kill so she decided she should speak up. "Please let the doctor do his job."

Setau crossed his arms over his chest, looked away from the doctor, and met her gaze. His fierce expression softened when he met her eyes and when he looked back at the doctor he nodded for the medical professional to continue.

The doc swabbed her arm and injected her with a painkiller. The pain lessened in seconds and she felt like she was floating in a boat drifting with the currents. She could hear murmuring but she was too tired to really listen and before long she drifted to sleep.

* * * *

Sab couldn't believe how right Zara felt in his arms. The painkillers the doctor had given her had been strong enough to knock her out, or maybe she had a low resistance to the medicine.

The moment the doctor had said they could take her home anticipation and excitement raced through his body. Although the others had been waiting for them outside and Pen had Zara's purse, Sab didn't feel that it was right for them to search her things for her address and keys, so they had decided to bring her home with them.

"How is she?" Set asked as he entered their shared living quarters.

"Still sleeping."

"That must have been some powerful shit the doc gave her." Set sat on the end of Sab's bed. Sab was leaning against the headboard next to Zara, who was still sound asleep.

"Has she been dreaming?" Set asked.

"No."

"That's good. The last thing we need is for the demonic to try and get to her when she's already hurt and vulnerable."

"They wouldn't dare," Sab growled. "We would know the instant they arrived."

"You're right. From what we heard Zara say, their shadow spirits are still too weak to manifest into solid beings. We'd be able to take them out with one strike from our swords."

"Were you able to contact Ra?" Sab asked.

Set shook his head. "He must be busy."

"Do you think he sent her to us?"

"I don't know, Sab."

"Do you want her as much as I do?"

"Yeah."

"I'm struggling to keep my fangs in check." Sab sighed and scrubbed a hand over his face.

"Me, too."

"The only time that happens is if we're injured and suffer great blood loss."

Set nodded.

Sab and the other sentinels weren't vampires but if they were gravely injured their fangs descended so they could replenish blood lost in battle. They ate food like any normal human being and loved being out in the sun. The only difference between them and a human was their strength, speed and enhanced senses. Plus the fact they were all immortal.

Sab was torn. He wanted Zara in his life—to hold and love her—but if he and Set did make her theirs, would she continue to age while they stayed the same? It would be torture watching her grow old and die.

Set had gone to Ra's temple to ask the sun god some very important questions but it looked like they would have to wait to get their answers.

He wanted to get to know Zara on a deeper emotional level but the yearning to make love to her was strong, too. His fangs erupted from his gums and his teeth throbbed along with his hard cock. Her sweet scent called to him on so many levels he wasn't sure how much he could take.

"Why don't you go and check on the others?" Set suggested. "You need to calm down before she wakes up. If she sees you like that you'll scare her."

Sab nodded and stood. He gave Zara a lingering glance before heading out. He paused in the hall. He really needed to get his urges under control. Mitry and Weni would tease him mercilessly if they saw him with his fangs out. Sab turned left instead of right and walked into the large cavernous room which had been set up as a temple to Ra. There were hieroglyphs on the walls and ceiling. The only surface not decorated with the art was the clear glass dome which let the sun's rays through into the underwater room.

He was glad that Ra had set this home up for them so long ago. He'd been bewildered when the deity had plunked them in Utah. Back then, there hadn't been anything but trees and fields, but the sun god had told them the demonic seemed to be very active in the area. Of course they were able to go to other parts of the country when necessary, but most of the time, they found themselves fighting close to home. When they were needed elsewhere, he and the other sentinels could get wherever they wanted with a thought. Sab thought it must be like teleportation, but he wasn't a scientist and didn't know about such things. All he cared about was being able to go where he wanted when he wanted—although to do so was very disorientating— and he much preferred to move under his own steam than with a thought. He hated the lightheadedness that seemed to follow every time he and the others moved like that.

At times it was frustrating chasing after the demonic, and although he was glad for their naiveté, humans never seemed to see what was right in front of their eyes. Utah Lake had been specifically made by their deity. The water was used to blend in with the clear pyramid of the glass and no doubt Ra's powers had a hand in their keeping their home hidden.

Sab knelt on the stone floor under the dome and sighed as the sun's rays replenished his weariness and fortified his control. His fangs receded and the tingling under his skin dissipated slightly. It seemed that nothing was going to help ease his erection but his own hand.

"That won't help either," Ra's booming voice startled him but he made sure he didn't flinch.

"What won't, my lord?"

"Masturbating won't ease the hunger."

Sab felt his cheeks heat. He'd never spoken about his sexuality with his god and was a little uncomfortable.

"Do you think I have never had a woman?" Ra's loud laugh echoed around the room.

Sab didn't want to think about Ra having sex and quickly pushed the thought from his mind.

"Is she ours?"

"Do you want her to be?"

"Yes."

"You need to keep her close. She has been chosen by one of Apep's minions."

Sab wanted to howl with rage, but he was able to swallow his anger. When Ra didn't say anything else, he chanced a peek from under his lowered eyelashes. A sigh of frustration escaped when he saw the room was empty. Although he hadn't seen Ra but for when he'd saved him and the others from being whipped to death, he always tried to keep his body in a submissive pose when in his god's presence. He was the only entity to see him in such a way because Sab didn't have a submissive bone in his body. Nor did any of the other sentinels.

He couldn't help but think back to the day Ra had appeared before him and Setau.

The crack of the whip hitting flesh made him cringe. He was walking behind Set, tugging on the thick rope as he and many other men dragged the huge square rock toward the second pyramid. It had taken years to complete the first triangular structure and although he was fitter than a lot of the other slaves, he was so tired he was scared if he closed his eyes he would never awaken again. Food was scarce and although they got to eat once a day, it wasn't enough to fill a mouse. The only thing that kept them going was water and the sound of that whip being wielded.

He cursed the pharaohs sitting in the lap of luxury with their bellies full as they gave orders for the tombs to be made. Why anyone would spend so much on something for when they died he had no clue and no doubt would never understand. The money they spent on having their monuments made could feed all the slaves working for them for an entire year and probably vastly more.

What he hated most was the way the overseers treated them. It didn't matter if you were young or old or on your last legs. If you weren't seen as pulling your weight you were whipped to within an inch of your life.

Each day his anger grew until he felt like he was consumed with rage. His inner turmoil grew hotter and higher with each passing second until he wondered if he would snap.

A cry of agony behind him had him spinning. The elderly man fell to his knees as the whip slashed across his back. Fury roared through him when he saw the man's back had been flayed open, flesh torn apart and blood dripping down.

Sab combusted.

He caught the whip in his hand, a howl of wrath emitting from his mouth. He pulled on that whip as hard as he could. Set roared and joined him, both of them taking the overseer down, fists pounding until their knuckles split. More overseers came running but Sab didn't care. He was in a berserker rage and took all of his anger out on as many men as he could.

He had no idea how long before he, Set and six others were taken down and although he knew he wouldn't live to see the end of the day, the carnage he'd left behind was worth it. They were dragged to posts and secured with their hands restrained and the light slave tunics they wore were stripped from their bodies.

Sab looked at each man who had taken a stand against the cruelty of their masters and nodded his thanks. They each nodded in return but that was the last he saw of them until he met them in the plain between life and death.

This time he was the man under the lash of the cruel whip and although he wanted to cry out in agony he didn't make a sound. Lash after lash ripped his flesh open and it took all of his will to remain on his feet. When the blessedness of unconsciousness beckoned he gave in to it willingly.

When he opened his eyes again he was surrounded by white fog, but there was no pain. Shadows moved through the mist and he was surprised to see Set and the other six men who had tried to help him save the old man.

"Where are we?" His voice seemed to echo off the fog but it also sounded suppressed.

"I do not know," Set answered.

"You are in the fade," a deep booming voice said. "The place between the living and the dead."

A huge muscular man stalked toward them and although he looked familiar Sab couldn't place him.

"You have a choice to make."

The man had a golden aura around him and it was in that moment that Sab knew he was a god. The glow around his head was bigger and brighter than the rest of his body. Sab drew in a deep breath and knelt with his head bowed.

"Ra," Sab whispered.

One by one the others knelt to the god in subservience. Sab had no idea why they were here but he didn't want to antagonize the deity.

"Yes," Ra said. "I need men like you. You are willing to fight against injustice and evil. If you agree to be my sentinels I will give you strength, stamina and speed beyond your imaginings. Your sight and hearing will be acute, and you will have immortality."

Sab wanted to ask more but didn't dare question the god.

"My nemesis Apep is the cause of all this greed and evil. His shadow minions have been hard at work. If you decide to work for me I will give you weapons that will dispel the demonic with one swipe. Your life will be long and lonely but you will never again lack for food and I will provide you with a home.

"You have a few minutes to discuss it with the others, but the answer you give will be final. There will be no changing your mind once you decide."

Sab didn't need any time to think things over or discuss his decision with Setau. He had always hated how the rich and powerful got away with anything they wished and if he could make a difference in the world and help his fellow human beings, he would.

He looked at Set and his friend nodded.

"I am Pentu Chatha. This is my friend Paser Ebo. We say yes."

"Nehi Fadil and I, Menna Jahi, agree."

"As do Mitry Mois and I, Weni Oba."

"Me too," Sab murmured to Set.

"Good," Ra boomed. "When you awaken you will be in a land far away. You will be healthy, muscular, and strong. You will need to train with the weapons I've supplied. The swords of Ra you will become proficient with and when I call you will come. You will have the ability to travel wherever needed with a thought and so much more. My command will be absolute and you will not argue."

"Yes, my lord," Sab answered. He didn't know if that was the correct way to address a god but when Ra didn't take umbrage with him he sighed with relief.

"Go and work hard, my demigods. Your rest won't last long."

Sab came back to the present when he heard Mitry's laughter echo down the hallway. He rose and headed toward the kitchen. Zara was going to be hungry when she woke up and he was going to make sure food was ready.

* * * *

Apep grabbed one of his demons around the throat the moment he felt a ripple of power surge through the earth into the bowels of hell. He lifted the sniveling prick from his feet, careless of the fact the idiot was clawing at his hands. He was used to pain and a few scratches weren't going to bother him. The moment his thighs met the cold stone of the altar, he slammed his minion down and with a wave of his free hand the demon become mortal. With a thought he called the long sacrificial dagger and plunged it deep into the minion's chest and then ripped it down through his body.

An evil laugh echoed through the underworld as Apep felt the demon's spirit rise from the body. He didn't care that the shadow was angry with him, all he cared about was getting rid of Ra's sentinels and seeking vengeance on the sun god. If it hadn't been for that fucker Apep wouldn't have been stuck in the bowels of hell for eternity.

He'd lost count of the times he'd tried taking out the sentinels with his shadow minions but since Ra had made them demigods they were impossible to kill. He'd come close a few times but close wasn't good enough.

Apep followed the trail of blood as it dripped into the brass bowl beneath the altar and when there was enough life essence he plunged his hand into the warm liquid and closed his eyes. This time when he laughed it was with glee and not maliciousness.

The moment he saw Setau and Sabu looking at the woman he knew that she would be instrumental in taking out the sentinels and no one was going to stop him. Not even the sun god, Ra.

Chapter Three

The moment Zara surfaced from sleep she felt the throbbing pain in her wrist and arm. It only took her a couple of seconds to remember why she was hurt and the men who'd come to help her. She frowned when she didn't hear normal hospital sounds around her nor smell the sterile environment she and many other people equated to that environment. And the bed she was lying on was way more comfortable from what she remembered when she'd had her tonsils out as a kid.

She held her breath when she heard a rustle and realized that someone was in the room with her. At first she thought it best to keep her breathing even and deep so that whoever was in here would think she was still asleep, but Zara had never been a coward.

She opened her eyes and peered about the dimly lit room, stopping her gaze near the left side and foot of the large bed she was currently resting in. Bright green eyes looked at her and she felt like she was falling into that gaze until he blinked and the spell was broken.

Making sure she was decent before she sat up, she was pleased to find that she was still wearing the clothes she had donned that morning before heading to work, sans the shoes. Using her left arm for leverage, she pushed up and scooted back against the headboard.

"How are you feeling?"

Zara licked her lips and nodded. "Okay. Where am I?"

Setau shifted in his seat as if he was uncomfortable but his gaze never wavered from hers. "We brought you home with us."

"And that is where exactly?"

"Near Provo."

"How the hell did you get me here? I don't remember anything." Zara glanced toward the door when it was pushed wider and saw Sabu walking in.

"Oh good, you're awake. Dinner's just about ready."

"Dinner?"

Sabu nodded. "Yeah, you were out all afternoon. That shot of painkillers the doc gave you must have been potent."

Yeah, and waking up every night scared out of my wits didn't help.

"I guess so." Zara glanced about as the two men watched her avidly. When she didn't see any windows and the amazing paintings on the far wall opposite the bed, she squinted. They looked like Egyptian hieroglyphs. That explained the different names. They had to be from Egyptian origin, but their English was perfect without the hint of an accent so maybe they had been born in America.

Zara grimaced when she moved her right arm. The throb had been an almost bearable dull ache, but now it turned into sharp piercing pain. She looked down at the cast that protected her broken bone, not remembering the doctor wrapping her in the plaster. Although it wasn't that heavy, it felt like it right now when the break was so fresh. No doubt by the time she was ready to get the cast cut off she would be used to it. It was going to be cumbersome and awkward for her to do things since her right hand was dominant but she would manage. She was so used to doing things on her own and the thought of asking for help…well, that just wasn't her. She was going to have to learn to do things with her left hand.

"You're in pain," Setau stated. "Sab, where are the pain pills?"

Sab reached into his pocket and withdrew a small clear bottle.

"I'll get you some water." Set rose and moved toward what she presumed was the bathroom. He came back moments later with a glass of water and nodded at Sabu.

Sabu tipped two pills into her cupped palm and Setau handed her the glass after she shoved them into her mouth. Moments later she handed the empty glass back to Setau.

"Thank you, Setau, Sabu." Zara pushed the covers aside and swung her legs over the edge of the mattress.

"Call me Set and him Sab." Set jerked his thumb to his friend.

Zara nodded and then shoved to her feet. She drew in a deep breath as the world around her swayed. Her wrist and arm throbbed. Carefully she brought her right arm up close to her chest.

"Here." Set gripped the elbow of her right arm, supporting her as she took a few steps away from the bed. "Okay." He nodded at Sab.

Zara turned her head to look at Sab and was pleased the wooziness in her head was gone. Sab held a blue piece of material with black straps attached to it and then he walked up behind her.

"The doc said you're to wear this for at least a week. It will help support and keep your arm still and having your wrist higher than your heart will help alleviate the pain." Sab reached around her from behind and maneuvered the sling into position before securing the straps. "Is that okay?"

Zara nodded. She wasn't sure if her voice would come out clear and concise right at that moment. The heat emanating off the two men standing so close to her was doing strange things to her body. When she inhaled deeply, she wished she hadn't. The aroma of sandalwood coming from Set had her body sparking with desire and when Sab moved from behind her, his cinnamon scent wafted to her nose. Smelling one of them was bad enough but now that she had the combination of their manly fragrances in her olfactory senses, she felt like they were consuming her and they weren't even doing anything.

Her pussy clenched, causing cream to drip out onto her folds and panties. She was damn glad she'd worn dress pants to work today rather than her usual skirt because she would probably have juices running down her thighs.

When she heard a low rumbling sound coming from Set she glanced up at him from beneath her lowered lashes and her heart stopped beating for a second before it slammed painfully against her rib cage. His eyes had changed from green to a glowing yellow hue and his lips parted as his canines elongated.

Zara tugged from his hold and ran for the open bedroom door. Fear skittered up her spine and rapid panicked breaths panted from her mouth. She was only a couple of steps from the door when a fast moving blurred shaped raced past her and the door slammed shut. She must have blinked because when she focused again, Set was standing in front of the closed bedroom door with his arms crossed over his chest and his legs shoulder width apart. He looked like he was ready to do battle and she knew she didn't stand a chance of winning if she went up against him.

She backed away and shrieked when she bumped into a warm, hard body. Her whole body shook as the fear racing through her veins tried to consume her, but if she was going down she wasn't going down without a fight.

Zara shifted, lifted a foot and although she knew she probably wouldn't do much damage the distraction might give her to edge she needed to escape. She brought her bare foot down on top of Sab's as hard as she could and then squeezed her eyes shut as shards of pain radiated up her leg.

"Enough," Sab growled and then she was lifted from her feet, up against his chest.

She wiggled, kicked, and flailed her left arm, landing a few wild hits and kicks but whatever she did didn't seem to make any impact. She froze when firm yet surprisingly gentle fingers gripped her chin.

"Stop fighting, Zara. We don't want you hurting yourself. Neither of us will ever hurt you, baby," Set said in a calm, soothing tone.

Her chest rose and fell quickly from her exertion and from her fear, but when she saw what looked like sincerity in his gaze, her breathing began to calm.

"What do you want with me? Who are you people?"

"Shh," Sab whispered. "We'll tell you everything soon, but right now you need to eat."

Zara decided the best course of action was to placate the two men for now. She would bide her time and when the opportunity presented itself, she would make her break. She relaxed her tense muscles and nearly sighed with relief when Set released her chin and Sab lowered her feet to the floor.

"Come out to the kitchen and we'll introduce you to the others." Set strode to the door, opened it, and walked out.

Zara followed, taking everything in as she moved. She walked through a comfortable living room all the modern conveniences and then out another door into a long dimly lit hallway. The walls were a bright blue color interspersed with the occasional hieroglyph and although she would have loved to stop and study them all, she didn't. She wasn't here to admire the art on the walls or the men, or whatever hell they were. She'd given in to get the layout of the place and find a way out.

Instead of following Set into the room he'd just entered, she stopped in the doorway and glanced at the other six men chatting. All eyes immediately moved in her direction and she tried to take a step back, but couldn't. Sab was right behind her and if she didn't want to touch him again, the only direction she could go was forward. After the last encounter with both him and Set touching her at the same time, she figured that moving away from him and Set was integral to her sanity and her libido.

Why the hell she was reacting to them when she had no idea what they wanted with her, she didn't know, but until she knew the answers to her questions she was going to make damn sure they didn't know that the mere sight of them turned her on.

A psychologist would have a field day with her if she explained she was lusting after her captors. She could practically hear the shrink's voice in her head. *You have what is called Stockholm syndrome. It's a natural defense mechanism in a stressful frightening situation where the captured becomes attached to the captor.*

Zara snorted and then ducked her head when the men looked at her speculatively. The room was big enough for her to skirt the outside without coming close to any of them, so she sidled along the wall, keeping them all in her vision.

"Zara, come and meet everyone," Sab said as he entered the room and walked toward the large dining table. She could see the kitchen part of the room across the other side and although there were dishes piled up on the sink from whoever had cooked, she could tell it was normally kept spotless. The appliances looked brand new, the stainless steel finish gleaming under the bright fluorescent light.

"Zara?" Sab frowned and held his hand out toward her.

He wasn't close enough to touch her but as far as she was concerned he was still too damn close. She didn't want to touch him again and shook her head as she pressed herself back against the wall.

The other men turned away and started loading their plates with food. Zara hoped that Sab and Set would do the same so she could run.

"There's nowhere to go, baby," Set said calmly as he took a step toward her.

"What do you want with me? I don't even know you. Please, just let me go?" Zara mentally cursed when moisture burned her eyes and although she tried to quell the tears they overflowed and trickled down her cheeks.

"You're in danger, Zara." Set took a step closer.

"No shit," she snapped, glad that his statement had turned her fear to anger.

"Not from us, honey." Sab moved along the wall. He stopped mere inches from her but didn't try to touch her.

"We know about the dreams, Zara," Set said in a quiet voice. "What you don't know is that those nightmares you're having aren't nightmares. They're real, baby."

Zara wasn't sure whether to laugh in his face or run from him screaming. Her heart was racing and her breathing escalated. "What?" she managed to ask after licking her dry lips.

"When you feel like someone is trying to tug your soul from your body. That's real. We are soul sentinels, Zara. It's our job to fight the shadows from the underworld and keep them from stealing a person's spirit."

Zara's legs were trembling and she wasn't sure how much longer she would be able to continue standing. She had no idea how these two men knew about her nightmares or how they played out, but then she remembered they had been in the diner the same time she had been that very morning. She'd told Mathilda about her nightmares and they had obviously overheard her.

"Good one, guys." Zara tried to laugh but it came out sounding a little hysterical. She looked for a way out but with both men on either side of her and the others sitting at the table, the way to the door was blocked. She spied a steak knife at the elbow of one of the other men and hoped she was strong enough to use it with her left hand.

She took a deep breath, pushed off the wall and rushed to the table, grabbing the knife in a tight fist and then quickly moved away from the table and the other men. When she looked back at Set and Sab they hadn't moved from their positions near the wall.

"You don't want to do that, honey. You could cut yourself." Sab stared into her eyes. She clutched the knife tighter and moved her arm up in front of her to defend herself against a possible attack.

"Let me—" Zara didn't get to finish because an arm wrapped around her waist and the knife was plucked from her grasp. The arm was removed and the heat at her back gone. She spun around to look daggers at one of the other men as he sat back in his seat. He smirked, winked, and then started eating.

Zara screamed loudly and long. She screamed out her rage, her fear, her confusion, and her lack of control. By the time she was done her throat was sore and her voice would no doubt be hoarse if she tried to speak.

"Feel better?"

Zara glared at Set, ignoring his question. If she hadn't just made a fool out of herself she would have screamed again. Set and Sab moved in to either side of her and without another word guided her to the table. She sat and stared at the empty place setting. If she hadn't had one of her arms in plaster and a sling she would have crossed them over her chest.

Set and Sab dished out some of the meat and vegetables onto her plate and filled her glass with water. She picked the glass up and drained it.

"Have you ever heard of Ra?"

Zara looked across the table at the man who had spoken.

"I'm Nehi, but everyone calls me En."

Although she didn't want to acknowledge him, her mom had brought her up to be polite so she nodded to him.

"Have you?" En prodded.

"Yes. He was an ancient Egyptian sun god."

"Is. I'm Menna. Call me Men."

"Mitry." He held his hand up. "Mit for short."

"Weni," he said. "Wen's the nickname."

"My name is Pentu but Pen is my normal moniker."

"I'm Paser. I usually do most of the cooking."

Zara glanced at each man as they introduced themselves. Although she still had no idea what was going on, the more time she spent with them the easier she felt. The fear was gone and she couldn't help but notice how handsome they all were, with their bronze and dark-colored skin and dark shades of hair. Each man had broad shoulders and ripped muscles from what she could see but the only two that could get a reaction out of her were sitting on each side of her.

"Ra stands up for the little people. He hates to see injustice, abuse, and greed." Set picked up her fork and shoved it into her left hand.

Zara looked down at her plate and saw that the roast beef and vegetables had been cut up into bite sized pieces. She glanced at Sab and he winked at her, before looking at her plate. "Eat, honey, I can hear your belly growling."

Zara put some beef into her mouth and moaned as the succulent juicy tender morsel filled her mouth with delicious flavor. She chewed quickly and swallowed before meeting Mit's gaze when he started speaking.

"Ra saved our lives. If it hadn't been for him we would have been long dead."

"That's true," Men said. "We would have been flogged to death."

"We stepped in when an elderly slave was whipped so bad the skin on his back was ripped to shreds," Pen said.

Zara could see the fury in his eyes and when she looked at the others they looked just as angry.

"Our masters didn't like that we'd stood up for one of our own," En said angrily. "We were about to be whipped to death, but the sun god stepped in after the first few lashes."

Set placed his hand over hers. She'd rested it on the table and didn't even notice she'd clenched it into a fist until his hand covered hers. Sparks of lust shot through her body and when she tried to tug her hand away, Set clasped her wrist, gently pried her fingers open, and threaded his with hers. Heat raced through her blood, warming her from the inside and she felt her cheeks warm, too. For some reason she knew if she tried to pull away again, he would let her and yet the thought of not having his skin touching hers made her feel empty.

Zara kept her hand in his loosely, not bending her fingers around the outside of his palm because she didn't want to give him any ideas, but when she met his gaze briefly and saw the desire in his eyes, she knew he already had lots of his own. She looked away and turned to see Sab was watching her intently and as she clenched her other hand into a fist she had to bite her tongue so she wouldn't cry out in pain. Sab must have seen something in her face because he placed his hand on her back between her shoulder blades and caressed up and down.

"Relax, Zara. You're safe here." Sab smoothed his hand over her shoulder and down her arm, being careful not to move the straps on her sling.

A shiver raced up her spine and although she tried to hide it she knew she hadn't succeeded when Sab gave her a sexy smile and winked at her. Zara needed to get control of herself and the only way she could think to do that was if she prompted the others to finish the rest of the story.

"What did Ra do?" she asked and mentally cursed when her voice cracked on the last word. She cleared her throat and then tugged at her hand so she could take a sip of water but Set didn't release her, and Sab half stood before shifting his chair even closer to her. Her mouth dropped open when Set lifted the glass and held it to her lips. "You can't be serious?"

Set raised an eyebrow but his expression remained stoic. His eyes never wavered as he tipped the glass against her lips. She had two choices. Open her mouth and swallow or keep her lips pressed tightly together and end up having the water dribbled down her chin and onto her chest. The bastard knew exactly what he was doing. She chose the first and swallowed the water but glared angrily at Set the whole time.

He took the glass away, placed it back on the table, and smiled as if he'd just won a huge victory and she guessed he had. He'd managed to bend her to his will without saying a damn word, but Zara vowed that would be the last fucking time she relented to his dominance.

Zara looked at Sab when he started to speak and she glared at him when she saw the gleam of amusement in his eyes, but he ignored her pique.

"Ra healed the elderly man and then with a flick of his wrist released us from the whipping posts and tethered the overseers to the poles. He berated them over how we had all been treated and then gave them a dose of their own medicine. He also stripped the pharaoh, giving the orders for all his worldly possessions to be distributed amongst the poor. When he was done he whisked us away to the fade, a place between living and death. After he made his offer to make us sentinels, he brought us to where we are now."

"Did you say pharaoh?" Zara closed her mouth when she realized it was hanging open and then swallowed loudly.

"Yes," Wen answered.

"How old are you?"

"We were enslaved to help build the pyramids," Mit replied.

Zara shook her head. That was over four thousand years ago. How the hell could they be that old?

"How old are you all?" she asked in a hoarse voice.

"We are nearly five thousand years old." Set squeezed her hand gently.

"But... How?"

"Ra made us immortal, honey." Sab shifted in his seat and turned toward her a little more. "We are what you'd call demigods."

Zara shook her head again. She couldn't get her mind around any of this. She felt like she was in a dreamlike state, but knew she wasn't asleep. Her mind was overloaded with information and she felt like it was going to burst open at any moment. She wondered if the stress of it all had made her blood pressure rise. It certainly felt like it, and she had a pounding headache. But what she didn't understand was what any of this had to do with her.

Chapter Four

Set could see the shock in Zara's eyes as she tried to process what they had just told her. He wondered if she believed them or if she thought they were all insane. He and the others could prove to her what they said was true but as her mates, he wanted her to trust that he and Sab would never lie to her. But he knew that they needed to earn her trust. He couldn't demand that she believe him after only just meeting him and Sab.

"What does any of this have to do with me?" Zara asked.

"We already told you, honey," Sab said in a soothing tone.

"What?"

"We told you that the nightmares you're having aren't nightmares at all." Set sighed. "The demonic shadows of the underworld have been trying to steal your soul, baby. If they steal a few souls their powers increase and they will be able to take over one of the bodies they are stealing spirits from."

"Why?" Zara's voice was more than a little panicked when she asked that question.

Set released her hand and slung an arm around her shoulders, pulling her closer against the side of his body. He felt the slight tremble of fear quavering through her small frame. She was scared and although he hated that she was frightened he hoped she would look to him and Sab to protect her. Hopefully as they grew to know each other she would agree to be their woman.

"The shadows only ever target innocent young women, baby," Set finally answered her question.

Her lips parted as if she were about to speak but she snapped it closed, her teeth clicking as they met. "I'm not innocent."

"Maybe not in mind," Sab gave her a gentle smile.

"This is crazy." Zara pushed Sab's arm off of her shoulders and tugged her hand from Set's as she pushed her seat back and stood. "You all should be in a looney bin."

Set watched her stomp from the room, his gaze zeroing in on her delectable firm round ass. He sighed with frustration when she disappeared from sight and slumped back in his chair. He wasn't worried about her leaving their home. The hieroglyphs on the door to the underground tunnel were protection spells. The only way for her to open said door was by her DNA being added to the glyphs and for her finger or thumbprint to be added to the security system. Only he, Sab, or one of the other sentinels could do that through the computerized system. Even if she accidentally left DNA on the door markings, she still needed to be added to the computer. Maybe letting her alone for a while was what she needed.

"So that went well." Sab sighed and scrubbed a hand over his face.

"She'll come around," Mit said.

"How do you know that?" Sab asked.

"She didn't actually refute what we told her."

"Mit's right." En leaned forward. "She believed everything we told her, but is having a little difficulty processing it all."

Wen nodded. "We've known about all of this for millennia. Humans think they are the only species alive on the planet. Being told otherwise would be a lot to digest."

"What I want to know is what she means to the both of you?" Paser asked.

Set sighed. Paser always acted like he didn't give a shit about anything but that was far from the truth and he was more observant than the others seemed to be. Although the other sentinels loved him like a brother, just as they all loved each other in their own quirky way, Paser usually kept to himself. He spent more time in the kitchen than anywhere else when they weren't out and about scouting for ripples of unrest in the human world.

"We think she's our mate," Sab answered before Set could.

The others stared at them with their mouths gaping open, but Paser leaned back in his chair, crossed his arms over his chest, and sat back with a self-satisfied smile on his face. That gave him pause because even though he was eighty percent positive that Zara was the other half to him and Sab, he still wasn't entirely certain.

"Have you asked Ra?" Men raised his eyebrow along with the question.

"Yes."

"And what was his reply?"

"The answer wasn't definitive."

"What do you mean?" Mit asked.

"His reply was cryptic." Set sighed with frustration. Although he loved and worshipped his deity, sometimes he wanted to shake him until he rattled. Of course he knew that if he ever got up the gumption to try such a thing, Ra would probably have his head on a pike.

Paser smirked but didn't say anything this time.

"So what are you going to do?" En asked.

"One thing's certain. We need to keep her close so that Apep's minions can't get to her," Sab said but his gaze was on Set's and he could see the same question in his eyes that En had just asked.

Set didn't know how to answer his friend because he had no idea himself. He wasn't used to dealing with the opposite sex. He'd had his fair share of women over his lifetime but he'd never been in a serious relationship. Ever. He'd never really had to work hard to get a woman he wanted, but he had a feeling that clicking his fingers like he usually did when he wanted sex wasn't going to wash with their mate.

He'd never been rejected by a woman in his life, but if he metaphorically clicked his fingers at Zara, he had a feeling she would slap his face, and rightly so. Until now Set hadn't realized how easy he'd had it. Maybe he would appreciate his woman more if she made him chase her. However, he didn't think that was possible.

Zara had the most innocent soulful brown eyes he'd ever seen and when she looked at him he felt like he was drowning in her virtuousness. She may not think she was innocent but she was. He could practically see the purity of her soul every time she looked at him and he was determined that Apep and his shadow demons would never touch her again. She was going to sleep between him and Sab each and every night whether she liked it or not. It was the only way they would be able to keep her safe.

Most women would be free of the shadow demons' pursuit once they lost their innocence, but there were a rare few who were so pure in spirit, so kind hearted and caring that losing their virginity didn't seem to make any difference to the demonic. Set was worried that Zara was one of those few. And if that was the case she wouldn't be safe until she was mated to him and Sab.

But first they needed to persuade her that they were the men for her.

And that was going to be a major task.

* * * *

At first Zara rushed through the long hallways willy-nilly, not taking any notice of where she'd come from or where she was going. She eventually slowed down and drew in deep ragged breaths, sighing with relief when her heart rate slowed.

Glancing about and trying to get her bearings as she walked through the rabbit warren hideout wasn't helping any either. She stopped when she came to large double metal doors which were covered in pictures of ancient Egypt and somehow knew that this was the way out, but there was no sign of a keyhole or lock on the doors and no way for her to open them. As she thought back over what she'd been told she wondered if the exit was somehow controlled by magic. They had told her they were demigods and if that was the case then she would never get out of here.

When a pang of reluctance seared her heart at that thought she delved a little deeper into her psyche and found that she was reluctant to leave Set and Sab. It was as if she had already formed a connection to them on an emotional level, but how could that be when they'd only known each other for hours?

Zara turned away from the door reluctantly and followed the long corridor to the end, taking note of the other hallways leading off of it and the closed doorways. Although curious about the doors, she didn't open them because she was worried about invading the other men's privacy. She would hate to think of some strange person exploring her room without her being present and couldn't do it to them.

She backtracked and took a right at the first T intersection and then took another right. There was a bright light coming through the open doorway at the end of the hall and she made a beeline for it. The moment she stepped into the room her breath caught in her throat. It was absolutely beautiful, the walls covered in the Egyptian hieroglyphs.

When she looked up she could see clear blue sky under a thin layer of water. She moved beneath the glass and was awed at the pyramid shaped dome that had to be at least twenty feet high and maybe twice that in circumference.

Zara wondered how the space could feel so warm when the water covered most of the glass but she stood beneath it and soaked up the sun's rays. She felt the turmoil in her mind lessening and the tension in her body began to drain. There was a peaceful tranquility in this room she'd never experienced before and wondered if this room had been set up by the men as a temple to Ra. Nothing would surprise her, she'd had enough of those to last her three lifetimes in the last couple of hours.

The tiled floor was terracotta in color and she thought that may have been done on purpose, to mimic the sands of Egypt which would have surrounded the pyramids back in the time of the pharaohs.

Zara tried to remember what she'd learned in history about ancient Egypt but she'd struggled to learn in that class. Her history teacher had been so damn boring, his voice an incessant monologue that droned on and on. She'd had enough trouble trying to stay awake in class, let alone trying to take in what was said.

She hated that she'd been a rebel back in high school but after her mother had died of brain cancer, her dad had gone off the rails. He'd taken to drinking to drown his grief, and since neither of her parents' parents had been alive, and she'd been an only child of only children, she'd ended up having to do everything in the home. When he came home ranting and raving it had taken all of her will not to snap back. She'd tried to convince herself that if she did everything at home and kept him as happy as possible he would eventually see her as the mature young woman she'd become, once he'd finished the grieving process. But that day had never come.

The last day she'd seen her father before he'd slammed out of the house she had seen pure hatred in his eyes when he'd looked at her and knew he would never love her like a father was supposed to love his child. She hadn't even realized how much her mother buffered her from her father's razor sharp, disparaging tongue until she was no longer there. The words he'd spewed at her would be forever etched in her mind and Zara knew that her father's hate for her had shaped her into the woman she was today.

"You look just like your fucking mother. You'll probably spread your legs for anything with a dick. I should have walked away when she told me she was pregnant. She slowly ruined my life and has been since the day we met. There is no way on God's green earth that I'm going to stay here and look after that slut's spawn."

Zara had been so shocked she hadn't known what to say and when his large hand slapped her face she hadn't so much as cried out. That hadn't been the only time he'd hit her but it had definitely been the last. She hadn't hung around to see if he'd come back because she didn't care. She'd been saving every penny she'd earned babysitting for the neighbors and their friends, waiting for the opportunity to leave without a backward glance.

She'd quickly packed her bag, grabbed the money she'd had hidden in a plastic bag under a loose floorboard, pocketed her cell phone and left.

Thankfully, her English teacher, Miss Rankin, had been really nice and Zara had known where she lived. She'd gone to her teacher's house and she'd arranged for Zara to board at another student's house. The Warren family had a small apartment above their garage and Zara had jumped at the chance to stay there until she'd finished school. She'd worked hard and ended up getting her diploma a year early and then she'd gone to college. Although the Warren family had left her alone and barely spoke to her, Zara had been grateful for their generosity. Miss Rankin had negotiated a fifty dollar reduction on the lease which had left Zara with enough money to pay for the small amount of food she'd needed to survive.

It didn't matter to her that the Warrens were rich and could have afforded to let her stay there for free. Zara would never have accepted charity from anyone. It had been hard and sometimes she would skip eating a few days in a row, but the struggle had been worth it in the long run.

The moment she'd graduated with her business degree, the sense of accomplishment had been overwhelming. It hadn't bothered her to see other graduates being congratulated by family and friends. The moment she'd held that piece of paper in her hands had been one of the happiest. She'd felt empowered for the first time in her life and knew that the world was her oyster. If she put her mind to it, she could succeed in anything she chose to do and she was determined to reach each and every goal she'd had since she'd been a child.

Zara felt a bone deep weariness wash over her and sank to her knees beneath the waning rays of the setting sun. She felt like she was in a living dream and yet she knew those men were as real as she was. What had her baffled though was they had believed every word they'd said and she was beginning to believe them, too.

The story they'd told of stepping in to save that poor elderly man from being flayed with the whip had been alive in her mind. She'd smelled the hot desert air, felt the hot sands beneath the thin sole of the sandals and she'd felt the fear and exhaustion weighing them all down. That was when she'd left the large kitchen dining room. All the emotions and the sensations had been too much for her to take, but it wasn't just the vivid depiction of their story that had scared her. It was the lust she felt for them and the heat she could see in Set's and Sab's eyes each time they looked at her.

Never had anyone looked at her with such hunger or emotion. Her mom had loved her in her own way but after her dad had left that fateful day so long ago, and recalling the words he said to her, she figured her mother had had secrets of her own. Zara had applied for a copy of her birth certificate before applying for college. She'd expected to see her dad's name on the paper but it had said unknown.

That had given her an understanding of her father she'd never had before and although her mom was never very demonstrative toward Zara, the woman who'd given birth to her had at least tried to keep her away from his vitriolic tongue.

Zara didn't know why she was suddenly thinking of her life when she had been growing up but suspected that this place of worship had something to do with it. She'd never been able to look back without becoming a little bitter about never being good enough but today she was able to look over her past with abject objectivity.

She felt so warm and comfortable she could have lain down on the floor and gone to sleep, but decided that when she did succumb to her weariness she wanted to be in a bed with a soft mattress and covers to keep her warm.

That thought led her mind back to Setau and Sabu.

Such unusual names but now that she knew their origin they weren't that strange. She liked that the men were okay with the modern shortening of their monikers since they were reportedly thousands of years old. She guessed living for so long it would be inevitable for them to have to change with the times. She couldn't even deem to consider what they had seen and been through and that gave her a new found respect for the eight men.

As she thought about them she wondered what sort of powers they had, since they had told her they were demigods. She wasn't naïve enough to think they didn't have any since they were all immortal. That thought gave her pause. She'd seen them eating food and suspected from the way this temple had been set up to expose sunlight, and the fact she'd seen them at the diner, that sunlight definitely had no effect on them, but what was worrying her was whether they were vampire like and if they needed to drink blood.

If that was the case, was she in danger of being a snack to the eight men?

She shook her head over that ludicrous thought. She had seen Set's fangs, and that had scared the holy hell out of her. But what if they only appeared or lengthened—or whatever—when they hungered for blood. A shiver raced up her spine but not a shiver of fear. That thought sent arousal surging through her body. When she shifted on her feet her pussy lips slipped together in the abundance of cream dripping from her and her panties were uncomfortably damp.

"You are one sick woman, Zara. Get a grip." A surge of power rushed through the room and she gasped when warmth enfolded her body. She turned in a circle to see who had entered but she couldn't see anyone.

"What you're feeling is natural," a deep booming voice echoed off the walls.

"What? Who are you?" Zara went to step back toward the door but her body wouldn't comply with her directive. She should have been scared out of her wits and screaming but for some reason she wasn't scared. In fact she was feeling as calm and tranquil as when she'd first entered the room.

"Who I am is not important."

Zara didn't agree with that statement but held her tongue.

"You need to be cautious, little one. You've been marked as a chosen."

"A what?" Zara quivered as a smidgeon of fear touched her soul.

"A chosen. You are one of a few who are pure of heart, mind, spirit, and body. The demonic aren't going to give up on you."

"What do I do?"

"Let your men mate you."

"Men? You mean Set and Sab?" She trembled at the thought of both those men making love to her. Her body responded with lust but she tried to push it away.

"Yes. Mating them will keep you safe. They will be connected to you in ways you cannot imagine. They will be able to follow you to the ends of the earth and beyond."

"I hardly know them," Zara prevaricated, trying to think of a reason to refute the invisible man talking to her.

"I will also be able to take you under my wing, young one. You can fight it as much as you like but in the end you will be theirs and they will be yours."

"Who are you?" Zara had a feeling she knew exactly who was talking to her, but didn't want to voice his name in case she pissed him off. She had no idea how to talk to a god and didn't want to end up being punished by him.

A deep booming laugh echoed through the room and washed over her. The laughter petered out and the extra warmth and power she'd felt before hearing the voice faded. Zara tried to move and was surprised and relieved when she could. Just as she entered the hallway she slammed into a hard, warm, muscular body.

Chapter Five

"Shit! Sorry. Are you okay?" Sab gripped Zara's upper arms to stop her from falling back on her ass. He'd been so lost in his thoughts he hadn't seen or scented her. Now that she was so close her delectable perfume seemed to wrap around his body, filling his lungs and nose with her aroma. His cock twitched and began to fill with blood. His gums itched and ached but he was able to stop his fangs from lengthening.

Set moved up beside him and looked Zara over, too.

She was paler than she had been and he suspected her wrist was hurting. Sab just hoped he hadn't hurt it when he'd knocked into her, but sighed when he remembered her left shoulder had slammed into his chest.

"Do you like the room?" Set asked.

"It's amazing. Did you all build this place?" Zara tilted her head as she asked her question.

Sab liked that little quirk she had going. It was such a feminine gesture and he wanted see more of her graceful movements. It had been forever since he and Set had been anywhere near the opposite sex, but he knew Zara was special and nothing like the women they'd hooked up with over the years. The innocence surrounding her was so pure he could actually see the light blue and white aura around her body. Only the truly special had colors like that. Other innocents he'd encountered had slight tinges of reds or oranges added into the mix, showing they had some dark tendencies. It wasn't that they were bad, because he knew most living beings were far from perfect, him included. It was just that Zara's soul was purer than any he'd seen in such a long time.

"No," Sab finally remembered to answer her question. "This is all Ra's doing."

When Zara took a step back Sab reluctantly released her. When she licked her perfectly full bowed lips, he hungered to kiss her. In fact he hungered to touch and kiss every inch of her, but he could tell by her body language she wasn't ready for that yet.

"What's he like? Have you ever met him? Does he have a loud deep voice?"

"He looks like any normal man, only he's tall and muscular," Set explained. "So I guess that answers the first two questions."

"And the third?" Zara's brows rose with her curiosity.

"His voice is quite loud," Sab said. "It seems to echo from everywhere and nowhere, but it's also very calming."

"Oh wow." Zara stumbled a step before she caught herself by placing a hand on the wall. Her other hand, the one in the cast had risen and was now on her chest over the upper slope of her cotton-material-clad breasts. Sab closed his eyes and staved off the groan wanting to emit from his mouth. Although she was properly covered with no hint of cleavage, his mind went into overdrive imagining what those lush feminine globes looked like. He wanted to know if the skin of her breasts was softer than the rest of her and the hankering to see the color of her nipples was almost overwhelming.

"Are you okay?" Zara asked and placed her soft, warm hand on his forearm.

Sab was speechless as he tried to get control of the tingling heat of desire running through his body from such a simple touch. A moan did escape from him as he imagined what her hand would feel like on other parts of his bare body.

Pushing his lust down was harder than he'd ever imagined, but he was able to when his eyes locked onto the plaster cast on her wrist and forearm. He was glad she didn't seem to be in as much pain as she had been ,and although she should have had the sling on, he wasn't about to berate her for removing it. In fact, he was surprised at how well she seemed to be doing where her broken wrist was concerned and wondered if it had anything to do with her being here, in their home.

Set nudged him in the side as he took a step closer to Zara. "Why did you say wow?"

"Huh?" Zara frowned, looking perplexed.

"When Sab explained to you what it was like to hear Ra's voice, you said, and I quote, 'oh wow.' Why?"

Zara licked her lips again. Sab shifted on his feet and surreptitiously adjusted his hard cock, pushing against the seam of his leather pants. He was glad she was focused on Set and hadn't seen the move, but knew Set was aware of his predicament when the corner of his lips curved up ever so slightly.

"Um…well…I think he spoke to me?"

"You heard Ra?" Sab asked.

"I think so, but I can't be sure. I never saw who was talking, but from what you explained his voice purported to be, it sounded like it could have been him."

"That's…amazing," Set whispered with awe.

"Why?" Zara asked.

"Because he's never spoken to a human before," Sab explained. "In fact he hardly ever speaks to us either. The only time we've ever seen him was when he saved our lives and just recently. What did he say?"

Zara glanced down at the floor and drew in a deep breath. Her face tinged with pink and she glanced up at him and then Set from beneath her lowered lashes. She shrugged and then sidled along the wall before turning and walking down the hall.

Sab was so damn curious about her reaction he wanted to race after her and demand she tell him, but he didn't think that would go over well with her. He met Set's eyes and saw his friend's gaze was glued to her ass. He was the one adjusting his hard dick seconds later.

"How the hell are we going to court her if she keeps walking away?" Sab asked.

Set frowned and shrugged before he started after Zara. Sab sighed and followed, but hope filled his heart when he realized that he could no longer feel fear and confusion coming off their mate. Did that mean she was getting used to them, getting comfortable with the idea of being their woman?

"Please, Ra, let her see how much we need her and how much she means to us already." Sab had no idea if the sun god had heard his prayer but he would try and do anything if it helped Zara decide sooner.

* * * *

Zara entered the large kitchen dining room to see the six other men playing cards. She walked into the kitchen but before opening the fridge to look for a drink she decided she should ask Paser for permission since she figured this was his domain. She walked up behind him and touched him on the shoulder. He jumped so hard the seat he was sitting on slammed back into her belly and knocked her onto her ass on the floor. As she jarred onto the hard surface she bit her tongue hard enough to draw blood.

"Shit!" Paser rushed over to Zara and knelt at her side. "I'm sorry, love. I didn't hear you come in. Are you all right?"

Zara nodded. Although her ass and tailbone felt bruised, her broken wrist was screaming in pain, and there was quite a bit of blood in her mouth. She wasn't about to swallow so much of the unpleasant tasting fluid. She accepted Paser's hand and clamped her teeth together as she rose. She knew Paser hadn't meant to hurt her from the contrite look on his face, so she wasn't about to take umbrage with him.

"What the hell is going on?" Set roared as he rushed over to Zara.

Sab hurried over as well. He looked her over from head to toe and then he sniffed the air. "I can smell pain and blood."

"Yeah," Paser said. "I'm so sorry, Zara. Where are you hurt?"

Zara shook her head slightly but she needed a bathroom bad. The blood in her mouth was starting to make her feel nauseous. She covered her mouth, hoping to keep the fluid behind her closed lips.

"Fuck, she's sick," Set snarled and then scooped her up into his arms. Zara didn't protest. She willed him to hurry and get her out of here before she made a complete and utter fool of herself by vomiting. "I'll deal with you later."

Set spun around so fast Zara had to close her eyes as dizziness assailed her. She didn't have them closed for long but when she opened them she was amazed to see that Set was entering the bathroom and lowering her to her feet. Zara shoved into the toilet, slamming the door closed behind her. She sank to her knees, raised the toilet seat, and spat the mouthful of blood out.

"Fuck," Sab said angrily from behind her.

That was the moment Zara realized she hadn't heard the door bang closed. She swiped the back of her hand over her mouth as she flushed the toilet and looked over her shoulder. Set and Sab were both crowded into the entry of the small room. She flushed with embarrassment at being the center of attention. She barely glanced at them before lowering her eyes to the floor.

"Get out," she said and winced when her injured tongue hurt. She moved toward them, intending to wash her hands and rinse her mouth out with water. Thankfully, the pain in her arm was now only a dull ache. She kept her back to them as she did just that and then turned in search of a towel. Zara wondered why her arm hadn't been hurting until she jostled it but quickly dismissed the thought when Set spoke.

"Not happening, baby," Set stated emphatically.

Zara looked up to meet his gaze and give him a piece of her mind, but her words flew from her head when she saw the fangs in his mouth. His eyes had taken on an ethereal glow. She backed up and gasped when her bruised ass hit the cupboards of the vanity. Fear surged through her body, tensing her muscles in preparation of the flight or fight mode as adrenaline pumped through her blood.

"Why are you scared?" Sab asked as he shoved Set aside. He glanced at Set and then looked beyond her to the mirror behind her. "Set, look at yourself."

"Wh... Fuck!" Set and Sab stepped back from Zara as they raised their hands in the air.

"Don't be scared of us, honey," Sab said as calmly as possible. "We would never hurt you."

"You have fangs." Zara pointed toward their mouths.

"Yes."

"Why? Do you drink blood?" She mentally cursed when she heard the quaver in her voice. What she wanted to do right then was run, but to do that she would have to go through them. And from what she'd seen at how fast Set was when he'd carried her in here, she didn't have a hope in hell of escaping them. They hadn't moved and she took a deep breath, holding it for a second or two before releasing it. As her fear dissipated she realized she wasn't really afraid they would hurt her. It was more to the fact that she'd been scared because they looked so different. The tension in her body eased and she leaned more of her weight against the counter of the vanity.

"On the rare occasion, yes," Set answered.

"When would that be?"

"In times of high emotion or in battle so we heal faster." Set lowered his hands and Sab followed suit. He took a step toward her, staring at her face intently and she guessed he was gauging her reaction to them after her scare. She held still except for crossing her arms beneath her breasts, mentally cursing the chunky cast. When Sab moved with Set she glanced over at him and when she saw his eyes were no longer on her face but on her chest, she looked down and saw that the shirt she was wearing was gaping and her cleavage was exposed. She uncrossed her arms and lowered them to her sides.

"Show me your tongue, honey," Sab demanded in a soft voice as he stepped so close she could feel the heat emanating from his body.

She had to crane her neck to meet his gaze. He and Sab were at least a foot taller than she was, if not more, and standing near them made her feel petite and feminine. She drew in another deep breath and resisted the urge to cross her arms over her breasts instead of beneath them this time. They felt fuller and her nipples were hard and aching. Her clit throbbed right along in time with her nipples and sent a fresh gush of cream onto her already soaked undies.

Zara parted her lips and then stuck her tongue out. It hurt quite a bit and although it felt like there was a big cut on it, she knew that the sensation was probably deceptive. The tongue was a very sensitive part of the body, just like the eyes were. She knew when she got dust in her eyes that the particles could sometimes feel as if she had boulders in them.

"Damn, that must hurt," Sab said as he stared at her tongue.

"That's quite a cut, baby." Set moved until his arm was touching hers.

She watched with anticipated trepidation as his hand moved toward her mouth. The moment his finger made contact with her tongue, she was lost. The flavor of his skin on her taste buds and the contact sent fire raging through her body. She squeezed her eyes closed and tried to keep her breathing deep and even but the task was beyond her. Her heart was racing, pushing her blood quickly through her veins and melting her insides. Liquid desire pooled low in her belly, making her knees trembly and weak.

"Do you want me to heal it for you?"

Zara's heavy lids lifted when she felt Set's warm fresh breath puff against her mouth after he'd removed his finger from her tongue. She pulled her tongue back into her mouth, swallowed around the dryness and nodded.

Set shifted from her side to stand right in front of her. His arm wrapped around her waist and he bent his head until his lips were pressed against hers. Without conscious thought her lips parted and he pressed his tongue in.

Zara had thought the taste of his skin had been good but that was nothing to what she was tasting right now. His tongue slid along and around hers and she moaned when she tasted desirable man mixed with something sweet and spicy. She clutched at the soft cotton of his T-shirt, the back of her fingers tingling when she felt warm rock-hard pecs. It was impossible to resist wanting to feel more so she straightened her palm and fingers, splaying them on his muscular chest. The heat coming off of him was amazing. He felt hotter than she did and his scent and taste was so intoxicating she wanted more. It wasn't until she heard a throat clearing that she remembered that Sab was also in the room. When Set had started kissing her she'd completely forgotten he was there, but now that he was in her mind again she felt a little bad for her neglect.

Set broke the kiss, lifted his head, and stared down into her eyes. She'd thought she'd seen him looking at her hungrily more than once before, but seeing him now had her heart stuttering in her chest. The raw desire in his gaze had her legs buckling and if he hadn't still had his arm around her waist she would have ended up on the floor at his feet.

She gripped his shirt again when he turned and then he released his hold and gently pushed her at Sab.

"I need to kiss you, Zara. I have to know..." Sab didn't finish whatever he was going to say, because in the next instant she was in his arms and he was kissing her passionately.

He tasted different to Set, but just as delectable and Zara wondered if she could pass out from such wickedly carnal intent. Her whole body was shaking and although she felt empowered she felt as weak as a newborn kitten.

She whimpered when his leg moved between hers and although her first instinct was to move her wet aching pussy over his thick muscular thigh, she restrained herself because she didn't want to come across as too needy, even though that was exactly how she felt.

His tongue swirled around and rubbed along hers, sending frissons of desire shooting straight down to her cunt. More cream dripped from her sex and she hoped they couldn't smell her lust. She moaned when a warm body pressed up against her back and without thinking about what she was doing she pressed her ass back against him.

She heard his sharp intake of breath and when he breathed out the warm moist air caressed her ear and neck. When he started nibbling on the skin just beneath her ear, she mewled with delight as she slid her hands down Sab's chest and over his washboard hard abs. Her fingertips dipped and glided over each delineation under his skin as she mapped his ripped muscles and when she encountered the waistband of his leather pants, she stopped and slid her arms around his waist.

Sab slowed the kiss until he was sipping at her lips and then lifted his head. The only sound in the bathroom was the heavy breathing coming from the three of them.

"You taste better than I ever imagined, honey. Thank you for letting me kiss you."

Zara didn't know how to respond to that because as far as she knew that hadn't been any of their intentions. Set had asked her if he could heal the cut on her tongue and then things had gotten out of hand. How, she had no clue.

"How is your tongue, baby?" Set asked, nuzzling his nose against her neck.

Zara rolled her tongue in her mouth and scraped it over her teeth. She was surprised that she didn't feel pain anymore and it felt as if the swelling had gone down. "Fine," she answered and quickly cleared her throat when her voice came out breathy and hoarse. "Fine," she said again, glad to have answered in a normal tone.

"Then it worked." Set stood up straighter and drew his arms from around her waist.

"What did?"

"Our kisses." Set shifted to her side, giving her a wink and a smile.

An ache settled over her heart and disappointment filled her soul. They had only kissed her so they could heal her tongue? Would they have even bothered if she hadn't been hurt?

Zara moved away from them and hoped her disappointment didn't show. When she got to the bathroom door she stopped and without looking back at them said, "Thanks."

She heard them curse but hurried through the bedroom. If they hadn't been in there she would have locked herself in the room until everyone had gone to bed, but she didn't know where she could go to be alone, other than someone else's room, but she wouldn't invade any of the others' privacy like that. So, decision made, she walked toward the sound of chatter and laughter coming from the kitchen dining room.

"Come and join us," En yelled over the others, patting the seat beside him as soon as she cleared the doorway.

Zara nodded, smiled, and hurried across to sit next to him.

"Do you know how to play poker?" Men asked.

"A little." Zara shifted in her seat when she caught the others staring at her mouth. She wondered if she had blood on her chin after she'd bitten her tongue, but didn't raise her hand to check. She didn't want to call any more attention to herself.

"How are you feeling, little one?" Paser asked, looking contrite.

"I'm fine. Don't worry about it. I know it was an accident. I'll make sure I stomp or something before coming up behind you."

"No need for that, love." Pen nudged Paser. "We hear and see a lot more than you could imagine. This one had his head in the clouds."

"Fuck you," Paser growled.

"No thanks, you're not my type. Now you, on the other hand…" Pen wiggled his eyebrows suggestively at Zara, making her laugh. That was until two angry snarls rent the air, causing everyone to stop laughing and turn to watch Set and Sab.

Set stormed over to Pen, grabbed the front of his shirt near his neck, and tugged him from his chair. "You will not go near her," he yelled in Pen's face. He was so close to his friend their noses were nearly touching.

"Hey, I didn't mean anything by it." Pen held his hands up at his sides in the classic "I surrender" stance.

Zara couldn't believe what an ass Set was being to his friend. The man had known Pen for thousands of years and here he was acting like a damn Neanderthal. She glanced at Sab and saw he was watching her with avidness. When her gaze met his he quirked his eyebrow at her in question and nodded his head toward Set.

She didn't need to ask what he meant because she just knew. Zara stood, pushed the seat back, and skirted the table. She tapped Set on the shoulder, waiting for him to look at her. He turned his head and frowned.

"What the hell do you think you're doing?"

Set gave her an astonished look before releasing Pen and glancing around for Sab. He made a rumbling noise when he saw his friend leaning against the wall with his arms crossed over his chest. "What are you looking at?"

"An ass," Sab retorted, then snickered.

Set turned and crossed his arms over his chest, trying to look all intimidating but it didn't work. In fact, his stance only seemed to make her angrier.

"Do you always treat your friends like that?" Zara poked him in the chest and he dropped his hands down to his sides and sighed.

"No."

"You're acting like a caveman, but I suppose since you were born in that era…" Zara trailed off for more effect and it seemed to work because Set scowled.

"Excuse me?" Set growled.

"You heard. What's with this, 'you will not go near her' stuff?"

Set shrugged and shoved his hands into the pockets of his leather pants.

"Do you think I'm a slut?"

"What? No!"

"So why did you go at Pen like that? Did you think I was going to spread my legs for him? Do you think I would do that for any of the others?"

Zara nearly smiled when she saw red creeping up his face and the muscles in his jaw started twitching. She was getting through to him.

"No," he answered quietly. "I'm sorry if you took…my aggression that way."

"You need to apologize to Pen, not me."

Set looked at Pen and sighed before threading his fingers through his hair. "I'm sorry, Pen. I don't know what came over me."

"Sure," Pen smirked before meeting Zara's gaze. "You're a tough little cookie, aren't you?"

"Um, no."

Mit stood, walked over to her, and slung an arm around her shoulders. "I like you. I hope you've decided to stay?"

Zara could feel Set's and Sab's eyes on her but didn't meet their gazes. She smiled up at Mit. "I like you, too." She gave him a playful hip bump but because he was so much taller than she was ended up bumping his thigh. "As to the other, that depends."

"On what?" Men shouted his question in a playful tone.

"On those two." Zara hitched her thumb over her shoulder toward Sab and then pointed at Set.

"You won't leave," Sab said as he came up behind her and wrapped his arms around her waist.

Zara looked up at him and hoped she kept her desire hidden when shivers raced up her spine at his heat, scent, and closeness. "Why do you say that?"

Sab bent down and whispered in her ear. "Because you like us."

Zara found herself nodding in agreement before she could stop herself and then muttered under her breath when Sab whooped it up.

"Shit."

Chapter Six

Set heard the exchange between Sab and Zara and although he wanted to whoop it up with his friend, he didn't. He felt like a real ass after Zara pointed out what a dick he'd been and wasn't sure him acting like a two year old would go over well just now.

Zara smiled as Sab danced around the dining area acting like a clown and he had to clench his hands into fists so he didn't go over to her and sweep her off her feet, carry her from the room and sequester her in the bedroom so he could have his wicked way with her.

She turned to face him and walked over to stand in front of him. He kept his demeanor relaxed but inside he was far from. She reached up and cupped his cheek and he couldn't stop himself from nuzzling into her palm, nor turning his head and pressing a kiss in the center.

"I'm sorry for being so angry with you." Zara dropped her hand and he wanted to tell her to put it back.

"You have nothing to be sorry for. I deserved everything you said. I was an ass. I…don't usually behave like this."

"Like what?" Zara asked.

"Possessive."

"You know I'm not a possession, don't you? I'm a human being and have feelings."

"Yeah," he answered quietly. "I don't have much experience with women."

"But you've lived for so long. How could you not have been with the opposite sex?"

Zara surprised him yet again when she leaned against him. He wrapped his arms around her waist and pulled her closer, being careful of her broken wrist. "I didn't say I hadn't been with the opposite sex, baby. Just that it's been millennia since I've had a relationship. So much has changed since then and I feel like a fish out of water."

"How long has it been?"

"About three thousand years."

"What? Why would you not want to be in a relationship?"

"I do, more than anything, but I'm immortal, love. Being one of Ra's sentinels has its drawbacks."

"Yeah, I guess so. I hadn't thought about it."

Set nodded in understanding.

"It must be hard on all of you. No wonder it's been forever. The women you've been with would have aged where you all stayed looking like you're in your low to mid-thirties."

"Yes."

"And they all died." Sadness washed over her when she saw sorrow in his eyes.

"Yes."

"I'm sorry."

Set squeezed her waist. "Again, you've nothing to be sorry for."

"So what happens between us if I decide to…accept your claim on me?"

"Claim?" Set queried.

"That I'm yours and Sab's mate."

"Oh. Well, I'm not really sure since I've never mated before but I presume the usual."

Zara ducked her head as her cheeks tinged pink but then she met his gaze again.

"But won't I grow old? How could we be…together if you…"

"What, baby? Don't shut me out now."

"You won't want to look at me, let alone…touch me."

"That's not true, Zara. The package on the outside has nothing to do with how beautiful you are. The most gorgeous woman in the world can still be ugly. You have a stunning inner beauty I've never seen in someone so young. Your soul glows with love, kindness, and innocence."

"Thank you," Zara whispered, blushing and she glanced sideways. "That may not be such a good thing, from what Ra told me."

Set tensed, clasped her chin, and tilted her head up. "What did he say?"

"That I've been marked as a chosen and that I was in danger." She swallowed nervously and he waited for her to continue. "That the shadow demons wouldn't give up until they got what they wanted."

"Fuck!" Set rested his head on the top of hers. She wrapped her arm around his waist and clung tight. This time when he smelt fear on her he knew it wasn't because of him or Sab. She was scared that the shadows in the underworld would get to her, but he was going to do everything he could to prevent that from happening. The best solution was to claim her and take a sip of her blood. If he and Sab did that they would be able to follow her anywhere. There was the added bonus of being able to feel her emotions, too.

When Ra had first turned them all into demigods, he'd shared his blood with them, which had started their transformation. After that had been complete he had ordered them to share blood with each other. Most of the time they blocked the others' emotions out except when they were fighting off the demonic. The only person he let in was Sab because they were the best of friends. That didn't mean he didn't have a strong friendship with the others, because he did, but he and Sab had grown up together and treated each other as if they were brothers. He couldn't imagine his life without him in it.

Now he was glad that he and Sab were Zara's mates because the two of them protecting her would have a better chance than if there was just one, but he was getting ahead of himself. Zara had to agree to be theirs before they could claim her.

Set was glad that the other sentinels hadn't heard their conversation, or if they did, it didn't show. He was happy that they had given him and Zara their privacy but now he needed to talk to them and discuss how to keep his mate safe.

He looked up and met Sab's angry gaze and knew his friend had heard everything he and Zara had said. Set knew his friend wasn't angry with him but at the circumstances. It was unacceptable that Zara was in danger and other than mating with her he wasn't sure what else to do.

"Are you hungry?" Set asked before kissing the top of her head.

Zara sighed and drew back. Set wanted to pull her back in his arms, but he'd made a start at getting to the heart of his mate and didn't want to stuff that up now by being too needy and possessive. Although that was exactly how he was feeling, he ignored it and let her step away from him.

"No, but I could use a drink."

"What would you like, honey?" Sab asked as he came up behind her.

Zara turned and smiled at him. "Whatever you've got."

"We have lots of things," Set said. "We have all types of alcohol, juices, tea, coffee, whatever you want is yours. All you have to do is ask."

"Do you have any chardonnay?"

"Yes," Sab replied and hurried into the kitchen. He pulled open a cupboard door to reveal a concealed glass-doored drink fridge which was packed full of alcoholic drinks. Set took the wine bottle Sab handed him and reached up into the overhead cupboard for a wine glass. He handed it to Zara, grabbed four bottles of beer, and headed to the table where his friends were finishing the last hand of poker. Sab brought another four beer bottles to the table and handed them out.

"Okay, did any of you hear what Zara said Ra told her?" Set asked as he sat next to his woman. Sab had taken the seat on her other side.

"Yeah, we heard," En answered.

"You did?" Zara looked around at the men and then quickly looked away when she started blushing. "That's going to take some getting used to. What else did you hear?"

"We weren't trying to listen to you, little one, we were too busy playing," Pen said.

Zara nodded and sighed with relief. Set didn't have the heart to tell her that all the guys had heard every word they'd spoken. She would realize soon enough how good their hearing was if she hung around long enough.

* * * *

Zara barely heard a word the others said as they talked about the demonic shadows and how to deal with them. She'd finished her glass of wine and only after taking the last sip, remembered that she'd taken pain medication earlier and probably shouldn't have had any alcohol. Her wrist was throbbing something awful and her fingers felt hot and cold at the same time. She was also beginning to feel sick to her stomach. Sweat beaded on her brow and upper lip and she clutched at the edge of the table when the world spun around her.

"Zara, what's wrong?" Sab placed his hand on her lower back and it was only then she realized she had leaned over until her forehead was resting on the cool wood.

"I don't feel so good." She moaned and clutched at her churning stomach.

"You need to rest," Set said as he shoved back his chair.

Zara groaned when her seat was pulled away from the table and she was lifted up against a warm, muscular chest and into strong arms. Just before she covered her mouth she managed to speak one word, "Hurry."

She closed her eyes when Set rushed out of the room at an amazingly ridiculous speed. If she hadn't been feeling so bad she would have laughed, but right now she was scared if she opened her mouth she would spew everywhere. She didn't think Set would appreciate her covering him in vomit and she didn't want to do that to herself either. When Set stopped she opened her eyes to see he was lowering her to the floor but he knelt down too and sat her on his lap. She wanted to tell him to get out but when she opened her mouth she was glad her head was already hovering over the open toilet.

Zara heaved until she had nothing left in her stomach. Her torso muscles were sore but it was her wrist that was plaguing her. The pain and heat coming from it was too much to bear and she suspected was the reason why she was feeling ill.

"What made you sick?" Sab asked as he reached over and flushed the toilet.

Zara hadn't even known he was there but wasn't really surprised. Sab and Set helped her to her feet and after she rinsed her mouth and brushed her teeth, she closed her eyes and stood swaying, feeling incredibly lightheaded.

"My wrist. There's something wrong," she managed to whisper and then groaned when she was lifted from her feet. The pain was traveling up her whole arm and was now digging into her shoulder.

"Fuck," Sab yelled. "Look at her neck."

"Summon Ra," Set commanded.

Zara didn't know what was going on but she had a feeling whatever it was couldn't be good. Not when Set and Sab were calling for the sun god. Whatever she had or was wrong was spreading and quickly. Her entire body was on fire and aching, and yet she felt like she was drifting in the skies. It was like her body and spirit were slowly separating. That thought sent terror racing through her mind and she thrashed, trying to push the hands on her away. She was being held down but didn't know by whom.

Images and nightmares plagued her. Glowing red eyes, dark shadowy figures and no matter how hard she tried to escape them, she couldn't. Zara felt like she was being consumed in darkness from the inside and she had no idea how to fight it.

Then all of a sudden peace washed over her and the image of Set's and Sab's faces were foremost in her gaze. Love she'd never known or felt filled her heart and she reached out toward them.

All her uncertainties about being theirs washed away and she knew in her heart without a shadow of a doubt that they were meant to be together.

* * * *

The moment Sab saw the dark tinge moving up her neck he felt stark terror invade his heart. He didn't know how, but he knew the demonic had somehow gotten to their mate. The moment Set ordered him to call for Ra he spun on his heels and ran as if his life depended on it, and since it was his mate who was in the grips of Apep's shadows, it may very well. He had no idea what would happen to him and Set after laying eyes on Zara, not that he cared for himself, but he loved his mate so much already.

He skidded on the sand colored tile floor, raised his head toward the pyramid shaped glass and prayed Ra would hear him. There was no sun shining down through the water and glass but he hoped there was enough light in the sky for Ra to hear him. Not once in the thousands of years of existence had Ra heeded a call in the dark hours of night, but he couldn't give up. Sab prayed like he had never prayed before.

"Please Ra, god of the sun, hear my call. My mate is being consumed by the demonic. I beg of you to save her. I don't know if I could go on if she were no longer by my side."

Sab felt Ra's power race over his skin but he remained on his knees and kept his head lowered. He would never presume to look into the face of his deity without permission.

"Rise, Sabu. We must hurry." Ra placed a hand on his shoulder and the room disappeared. When his blurry vision cleared he was kneeling by the bed that Zara was lying on. He pushed to his feet, sat on the edge of the mattress at her side and took her small fragile hand in his. Set had her head cradled in his lap and was stroking her hair.

"Keep your hands on her," Ra commanded. He moved closer to the bed, kneeled on the mattress and placed his hands on her body. One on her forehead and the other on her stomach.

Sab held his breath when Ra's hands began glowing. Zara moaned and tried to roll away but with the three of them holding her down, she didn't stand a chance. When her body grew taut and she shuddered beneath their touch, he gritted his teeth against the fury and fear he wanted to bellow to the skies.

The light coming from Ra's hands was so bright he had to close his eyes, but he kept a firm hold of Zara's hand and the other on her thighs. He could hear Ra chanting or muttering but it was in the language of the ancient gods and he couldn't understand it, but he could feel the raw power emanating from his deity.

The tension began to ease when he saw the dark tinges diminishing and the paleness of Zara's face receded, returning to a more normal color. He wasn't sure their mate was out of the woods yet, but at least whatever had been spreading through her system was waning.

Sab opened his eyes when Ra spoke. His loud deep voice seemed so much more in such a confined space. "One of the demonic managed to poison her."

"How?" Set snapped out his question. "She's been here with us the whole time. Those fuckers aren't able to get in here either. You made sure of that."

"Has she eaten or drunk anything?"

"The only thing she's had that we haven't is a glass of wine." Sab answered.

"Get it."

Sab raced from the room, grabbed the nearly full bottle of wine from the counter, and raced back. He didn't have to look back to know that the others were following him. The moment he stepped back into the room, Ra took the bottle from him, lifted it to his nose, and sniffed.

"This is tainted," Ra said and then looked over at Zara before meeting everyone's gaze. The others were crowded just inside the doorway.

"What's going on?" Paser asked. "What's wrong with Zara?"

"She's going to be fine, now," Ra answered. "You need to stop getting your food and drink delivered. The shadows won't be able to poison your supplies if they don't know where you're going to get it from. Make sure you go to different stores and don't go on the same day when you do go out to buy things."

"You think one of the demonic has managed to take over a human?" Mit asked.

"That's the only possibility. They can't use their powers from the underworld to taint things, only people, but only if they've stolen part of the human's soul."

"When is this shit going to end?" En asked as he ran his fingers through his hair. "I'm getting sick of fighting Apep's minions all the time."

Ra crossed his arms over his chest, but he nodded at En. "I know, but as long as Apep is in existence there will always be a need to fight. However, you will all be rewarded for your loyalty and care of the humans."

"How are you going to—" Mit began to ask but Ra cut him off.

"You will all find your mates." Ra smirked when Mit's mouth dropped open with astonishment.

The sun god turned back to the bed and placed his hand on Zara's forehead. "Let you mate sleep through the night. When she awakens all will be well." He moved his hand from her brow and placed it on the plaster cast covering her wrist and lower arm. The plaster disappeared and Sab watched in awe as the swelling went down and the bruising vanished. Sab looked at Ra when the deity straightened. "The break is no more."

Ra walked toward the door and eyed the other sentinels with what looked like satisfied glee. Sab wanted to ask, but decided if the sun god wanted them to know things then he would tell them. Sab didn't have to wonder for long.

"When you claim her, mark her by taking some of her blood." Sab and the others didn't get to ask Ra any questions, because he was gone before he could open his mouth. He glanced over at Set but his friend was staring at Zara.

The others began leaving and as Wen was closing the door behind him, he met Sab's gaze. "You're lucky you found her first. If I had, she would be mine already."

Sab took a step toward his friend and growled but Wen quickly shut the door. His chuckle of mirth had him realizing he'd just been baited and caught. He turned back to the bed, stripped down to his boxers and climbed into bed next to Zara.

Set rose, did the same, and got in on the other side of their mate. Zara sighed and turned onto her side, snuggling up to him as she draped an arm over his waist and rested her head in the crook of his arm and chest.

Set shifted until his front was pressed to Zara's back and he wrapped an arm around her waist. "Do you think she'll accept us?"

Sab lifted his head to meet his best friend's gaze. He was feeling very optimistic so he smiled and nodded, before lowering his head back to the pillow.

"I hope you're right, Sab."

"Ra wouldn't have sent us to her if she wasn't perfect for us."

"Yeah, but we've had thousands of years to deal with this shit. Zara's only really had just over twenty four hours."

"But she's handling it well."

"Way better than I ever expected," Set said.

"As much as I hate that she's been dealing with the demonic in her sleep, I think that helped her to accept everything. Plus, Ra talking to her facilitated things."

"Do you think she'll freak when we tell her we have to drink a bit of her blood?"

"That's a good question, but we won't be able to get the answer till the morning." Sab kissed the top of Zara's head and ran his hand down her thigh. He had wanted to strip her clothes off but didn't feel right doing that to her when she wasn't conscious. They were going to need to take her home to pick up her things, or take her shopping for something to wear.

Since nothing could be done or answered now, Sab relaxed his body, slowed his breathing, and tried to sleep.

Hopefully tomorrow they would have more answers.

Chapter Seven

Zara sighed and stretched her cramped muscles, then immediately stilled when she felt warm, hard bodies on either side of her. She didn't remember coming to bed and she wondered why she was still in her clothes.

Her eyes popped open and although she was surprised to find them in bed with her, she wasn't surprised to see that it was Sab and Set. Set's eyes were open and he was scrutinizing her face. He must have felt her tense or heard her deep inhalation because he lifted his gaze to hers.

"How are you feeling, baby?"

"Fine." She frowned when she saw the concern lingering in his eyes.

Sab snuggled in her back, nuzzling his nose against the sensitive skin just below her ear. "Do you remember what happened last night?"

It took her a few moments to remember feeling sick to her stomach and the excruciating pain in her wrist and arm. She knew she'd vomited but everything was hazy after that.

"My arm was hurting bad and I got sick." Zara tried to recollect more but nothing else would come. "I wasn't sick on you two, was I?"

"No, honey, but we had to call Ra to heal you." Sab shifted up onto his elbow.

Zara pushed herself up until she was leaning against the headboard. "You did? Why?"

"The wine you drank was cursed," Set moved until he, too, was sitting against the headboard.

Zara's mouth nearly dropped open when she saw the muscular expanse of his bare chest. He was so toned his pecs looked like they would have no give if she dared to reach out and touch him, and although she refrained it was a near thing. Her arm was already moving toward him, but she stopped herself before it was too late.

"My wrist doesn't hurt." She waved her arm and flexed it. The bruising and swelling were no more, and the cast was gone. Nothing she did caused any pain. When she realized what Set had said she stared at him before glancing at Sab as he too, pushed further up the bed. "What do you mean the wine was cursed?"

"One of the demonic shadows has to have escaped from the underworld and taken over a human body. We get our food and drink delivered from the same place every week. The demon must have found out where we placed our order and tainted the wine," Sab explained.

"So they know where I am?" Zara swallowed as she looked Sab's chest over. Both men had a familiar tattoo on their upper left pecs. When she looked at Sab's mark and then Set's she was sure that there was a faint golden glow to their skin.

Set shifted until he was turned toward her and cupped her cheek. His gaze was full of determined intent and she felt a little of her fear wane. "We won't let them get you, baby. They'll have to go through us first."

"How can you promise something like that? You can't invade my dreams and keep those…things out."

"Actually we can." Sab moved a little down the bed, kneeling next to her hip and facing her.

"How?"

"If you agree to mate with us we will be connected to you at all times," Set explained.

"How is that possible?" Zara frowned, not sure what he was talking about.

"Ra told us that we will need to bite you and mark you. He didn't say anything beyond that but just before Ra left, our minds were flooded with information." Sab reached out and clasped one of her hands.

Set took up where Sab left off. "We will need to drink a little of your blood."

Zara didn't even know she was going to move until she was off the bed. She'd had no idea she could move so fast.

Sab slowly got off the bed and took a step toward her but stopped when she held up her hand, warding him off.

"You drink blood?" Zara hated the way her voice trembled but after seeing their fangs she began to wonder if they were vampires after all and had lied to her.

They had told her all this before, but she couldn't get her mind around them taking blood from her. The thought just totally grossed her out, but not because they would have to bite her. That thought sent desire humming through her body. What grossed her out was the fear that if she mated with them, she would have to drink blood, too. She was scared (not really), and she knew they would hurt her. However, she was anxious over the fact of them drinking her blood and draining her dry. Even if they didn't mean to. She'd read some erotic romance stories about that sort of thing happening, and since she didn't know them very well, she was trepidatious.

"No," Set answered as he rolled from the bed and came to stand beside Sab. "Not the way you mean, anyway."

"Explain it to me then." Zara bit back a gasp of hunger when she noticed Set was only in a pair of boxers. She tried to keep her eyes from wandering, but she couldn't seem to help herself. Both he and Sab were so damn—muscular and sexy. Her gaze landed on his crotch, and she crossed her arms when her nipples hardened, hoping neither of them had noticed.

"If you allowed it and accepted us as your mates, while making love to you we would bite at the curve of your neck and shoulder and take a small sip of blood. We would be connected to you on a very deep level. Our emotions would be yours and yours ours. We would be able to find you at the ends of the earth and we will also be able to communicate with you in our minds." Set took another step forward so that he was within touching distance.

"Our souls would be bound together for eternity, Zara," Sab said in a quiet voice.

"Are you telling me that I would be like you are?"

"Not quite." Set sighed and scrubbed a hand over his face.

Zara's heart clenched when she saw uncertainty in his gaze as he met her eyes again. To see such vulnerability in a strong, dominant man made her fall for him a little more, and there was no doubt in her mind or heart that she had started to care for them from the moment they'd helped her up from the pavement.

"You would be stronger, healthier, heal faster and your senses would be enhanced. You won't get fangs that I know of, although that's a possibility, but you will also live as long as we do. I don't know all the facts other than what Ra allowed us to, and knowing him, he left out information on purpose. I'm sure we don't know everything and add in the fact I've never been mated before...your guess is as good as ours."

Zara's mind was spinning with questions. There were so many things she wanted to ask but the first and foremost was something she'd dreamed about since she was a little girl. "Will I be able to have children? And if I am, will they stay babies or will they grow at the same pace as a human child?"

"Yes and yes," a deep booming voice echoed around the room, making her jump. She squealed and threw herself into Sab's arms, sighing with relief when he caught her and lifted her against his chest.

"Geez, give a girl a bit of warning next time, Ra." Zara felt Sab tense but when Ra boomed out a loud laugh he relaxed again.

"Stop delaying the inevitable, Zara Barry, and let them claim you. They are already in your heart."

Zara ducked her head, hiding her face in Sab's neck as a blush stole up her cheeks. She was going to have to have words with the sun god and tell him to keep his mouth shut. There were some things that a girl just needed to keep to herself and how she felt about Set and Sab was one of those things. At least until she was ready to speak of what she was feeling herself.

"You're right, Zara. I'm sorry. I will leave you to deal with your mates," Ra said.

"Keep out of my damn head," Zara muttered.

Set placed his hand on her shoulder. "You really shouldn't talk to Ra…"

Ra laughed again. "I like you, human. The sentinels need to take a page out of your book. Till we talk again."

The hair on Zara's arms stood up and a surge of power washed over her and then faded. She knew that the sun god was truly gone this time.

"What did he mean by that?" she asked, looking up at Sab.

"I think he meant that we treat him with such deference that he was refreshed by your bluntness and honesty." Set gave her a chagrined smile.

"Oh."

"You are special, Zara," Set said in a whisper.

"No, I'm not."

"You are." Set nodded. "I can count on one hand the amount of times Ra has spoken to us over the last five thousand years, and he only appeared to us twice in person. One of those times was right before we met you. Now he's talking to you and popping in whenever he likes. It's…astonishing."

"So is what he said true?" Sab asked impatiently. Zara could hear hopefulness in his tone.

"About what?" She hedged and stepped from between them, hoping to get away from them before they saw how hard her nipples were. She nearly stumbled when she remembered them telling her about their enhanced senses and hoped they couldn't smell her arousal.

"You know exactly what I'm talking about, honey."

Zara stiffened when a muscular arm wrapped around her waist and she was pulled back against a warm hard body. She moaned when she felt the ridge of his hard dick pressing against her lower back and although she tried to remain still, she was fighting a losing battle.

She hadn't even noticed she'd closed her eyes until Set palmed her cheek. Her lids lifted and she stared up into his hungry gaze. "You can fight and deny it all you want, but we can smell the need on you, baby."

Zara licked her lips and when he lowered his head down to hers it took everything she had not to grip the back of his head to make him move faster. She whimpered with excited anticipation when his soft lips brushed over hers and then nearly growled with frustration when he began to speak.

"Say yes, Zara. Tell us you'll mate with us. Tell us that you'll let us mark you and spend eternity with you, loving you," Set demanded.

She closed her eyes for a brief second and knew the moment she opened them again he could see the answer in her gaze.

"Tell me," he commanded.

"Yes," she whispered.

Set opened his mouth over hers, his tongue pressed between her lips and teeth and she was lost. Lost in his taste, touch and need for him and Sab. His tongue twirled around and then rubbed along hers before he explored every inch of her mouth.

Sab pushed one of his hands beneath her shirt, caressing her belly and moving up toward her chest. She moaned and then whimpered when Set drew her tongue into his mouth and began sucking on it. She went up in flames, liquid heat coursing through her veins until she felt as if she was about to melt into a puddle.

A groan of pleasure erupted from her when Sab cupped her bra-clad breast as he began to nibble on her neck, but was muffled by

Set's mouth. Her knees buckled when Set's hand delved into her panties and cupped her wet pussy, the only reason she remained upright because of Sab's arm around her waist.

The moment Set lifted his mouth from hers, she wanted it back. She was already reaching for him when Sab scooped her off her feet and carried her to the bed. He gently placed her on the mattress and began to remove her clothes. When she was naked both men shucked their boxers and got up beside her. Her breathing was shallow and fast but she couldn't regulate it. Not when there were two god-like specimens of masculinity right beside her and they were hers. Hers to touch, kiss, and love.

Zara's heart filled so fast and full with warmth it felt like it was about to overflow. It didn't matter anymore that she'd known these two handsome, sexy men, demigods, sentinels—whatever—for only a few short hours. What mattered was that she listened to her heart and body. Her body knew what it wanted and had never reacted this way to any other man in her young life, and neither had her soul. They felt right and made her feel complete in ways no other person ever had and she wasn't about to walk away and spend the rest of her life wondering "what if."

All that was left to do was to complete the mating and she would know for sure how they felt about her. And even if they didn't care for her as much as she did for them, consequences be damned. She would deal with that later because right now she was so hungry, needy for them she felt as if she would die if they didn't make love to her.

Set leaned over her, cupped her face, and then bent until their lips were pressed together. She opened to him without any hesitation and moaned as his tongue glided along hers. She kissed him back just as passionately as he was kissing her. He tasted so good. He tasted of passion and man and she couldn't get enough.

When her lungs began to burn she broke the kiss and gasped for air and then she was gasping for another reason. Sab pushed her legs apart and smoothed his hands up her thighs until his thumbs were on her pussy lips. She groaned at the pleasurable sensations and then whimpered as his fingers slid between her folds, spreading the cream leaking from her cunt up to her clit.

"You're so fucking wet," Sab said in a growly voice. "I need to taste your honey."

Zara drew in a deep ragged breath and closed her eyes when Sab hunkered down between her legs until his head was hovering over her pussy. Her eyes snapped open again when Set swirled his tongue around her nipple over the areola until the skin puckered and her nipple hardened even more.

A cry of pure pleasure left her mouth when Sab lowered his head, laving the tip of his tongue over her clit, causing her pussy to clench and more juices to weep out. When Sab pushed a finger up into her wet cunt a guttural sound formed in her chest and emitted from between her parted lips.

She'd never felt anything so exquisitely blissful in her life and he was only stroking a finger in and out of her pussy. She couldn't imagine how wonderful it was going to feel once he had his cock in her vagina.

Set released the nipple he'd been sucking on and kissed her lightly on the lips. "Do you like what Sab is doing to you, baby? Do you like how it feels when he licks your cunt and finger fucks you?"

"Yes," Zara moaned and groaned when Sab drew her clit into his mouth. Cream was continuously leaking from her pussy as he drove a finger in and out of her sex. It felt so damned amazing but she wanted one of her men to fill her cunt with their hard cocks.

Using the hand closest to Set, she placed it on his washboard abs and caressed down. The tip of her finger brushed against the damp head of his cock and her mouth watered for a taste. She wanted to know what his cock tasted like, needed to know if his pre-cum was salty or sweet or maybe a combination of both.

She reached down more and wrapped her hand around his hot and hard, yet surprisingly velvet-soft skinned erection. He moaned and shoved his hips toward her and when she adjusted her grip on him she realized that her fingers didn't meet. He was so damn big and sexy all over and although she was a little trepidatious about his and Sab's size, she wasn't about to let a little nervousness stop them from claiming her. She hungered for them to fill her, for them to relieve the ache that had been growing stronger and more intense since she'd first spotted them walking into the diner.

The heat coursing through her veins got hotter and when Sab added another finger to her pussy and began driving them in and out of her faster and deeper, she felt as if she would melt right into the mattress.

Zara pumped her hand up and down Set's cock, relishing the soft covered steel moving against her palm.

"That feels so fucking good, baby," Set rasped. "Squeeze me harder, Zara."

Set covered her hand and showed her how he liked to be stroked and she complied, wanting to give him as much pleasure as they were giving her.

When Sab pressed against a really sensitive spot inside of her at the top wall of her cunt, she cried out and arched up into his mouth. He made a growly sound and slurped at her cream and each time his fingers stroked in and out of her pussy, he made sure to rub that sweet spot. The tension built inside, her internal walls seeming to gather closer and closer together as the friction of his rubbing digits created pleasurable friction along her wet flesh, until she was hovering on the precipice of something so big she began to shake.

"Let go, baby. Don't fight the feelings, we won't let you fall. We'll catch you, Zara. Now come!" Set slanted his mouth over hers, kissing her rapaciously as he cupped both her breasts in his hands and then tweaked her nipples between his fingers and thumbs.

That, and the way Sab was stroking that spot inside her cunt as he flicked and sucked on her clit sent her screaming toward the heavens.

Bliss held her in its grip, her pussy pulsing and contracting around Sab's still moving fingers as he sucked and licked at her clit. Her body quaked and quivered, juices gushed from her cunt and her limbs trembled.

She writhed and thrashed in the throes of a powerful orgasm, hearing a roaring sound in her ears and she saw stars flash before her eyes.

Zara had no idea how long the climax lasted and although it felt as if minutes had passed she knew it had to be only seconds. The tension seeped from her muscles and she panted for breath as she came back to herself, trying to get her equilibrium back under control.

She hadn't even noticed that Sab had removed his fingers from her pussy until the mattress between her legs dipped as he shifted. She opened her eyes to see that he was up on his knees pumping his hand up and down his hard cock. She glanced at Set to see that he was doing the same and licked her dry lips.

"I love watching you come, honey, but next time is going to be with me inside of you." Sab gave her a heated look.

"Did you like that, baby?" Set asked as he caressed a hand over her belly, up to her breast to knead and mold before smoothing his hand down to the top of her mound.

"Yes."

"Are you ready for more?" Sab asked, rubbing his fingers over her hips bones.

"Yes."

Chapter Eight

Sab licked his lips, savoring the taste of her delicious cream on his tongue before swallowing it down. He still couldn't get over how sexy Zara was when she was coming and pride filled his chest that he'd had a hand in giving her what seemed to be her first orgasm. Or maybe it was the first time she'd come when not from her own hand. He'd seen the surprise in her eyes just before she'd tipped over the edge and he wanted to see it again, but this time he wanted her coming around his cock.

Set was currently licking and nibbling on her neck and although Zara had her hand wrapped around his friend's cock she got so caught up in the sensations they were bestowing on her, she stopped pumping him before she started up again. He could see the hunger in Set's eyes whenever their gazes met and a couple of times he looked like he was being tortured, or was that tormented with pleasure?

Sab couldn't wait for Zara to touch him the way she was Set and he didn't care if she forgot to move her hand because she was ensnared with pleasure. What he really yearned to do though was to flip her over and fuck her ass while Set fucked her cunt, but after just making her come and seeing the amazement on her face as she came, he knew she wasn't experienced in the lovemaking department and he didn't want to scare her off by becoming too aggressive and needy.

Set reached her mouth and started to kiss her hungrily while he pinched and plucked at her nipples. Sab looked down at her cunt and saw her little pussy hole flex and cream spilled out before dribbling down to cover her anus. Seeing her sexy body pulsing with famishment to be filled by his cock had him nearly tipping over the edge. His balls felt as if they were rock hard and were high up against his body as if he was about ready to shoot his load, and he wasn't even inside of her yet. He released the base of his cock, grabbed hold of his testes and scrotum and gave them a light yank down. The small bit of pain was enough for him to get his lust back under control and the pending orgasm from receding, but he wasn't sure how he could take much more. Especially since he still had the delectable taste of her sweet honey on his tongue.

Sab drew in a couple of deep breaths, releasing the air from his lungs slowly and then he gripped the base of his cock again. This time instead of pumping his hand up and down his erection, he aligned the head of his dick with her cunt and began to push in. He was careful and took his time because Zara was so fucking tight as he stroked his cock deeper into her. The grip her cunt walls had on the inch he had inside of her was almost painful.

Set released her lips, shifted further down the mattress and once more began sucking on one of her nipples. Zara made little moaning sobbing sounds as Sab slid in another inch, but from the expression on her face he knew he wasn't hurting her. He had been watching her from the moment he'd pressed the tip of his cock against her cunt and when he hadn't been able to see her face because Set was kissing her, he'd watched her body language.

"Oh," she moaned and bucked her hips up as if she couldn't wait for him to get all the way inside of her, but since he didn't want her hurting herself, he grasped her hips and held her to the mattress.

"Do you like that, honey?" Sab asked between panting breaths. His muscles, body was so pumped with excitement and blood he had to make sure to keep a tight rein over his control. He felt as if he was only hanging on by a thread.

"Yes. More. Please?" Zara gasped.

"I need to take things slowly, Zara. I don't want to hurt you."

Zara's hand landed on his chest and caressed over his pecs and up to his shoulder. "You won't. I trust you."

Her whispered words were like a balm to his ego, but still he was taking it easy on her until she'd adjusted to his penetration. If he hurt her she could end up with psychological damage in regards to sex and he never wanted to be the cause of something like that. Ever. And especially not with his mate.

"Just relax, baby." Set met Sab's gaze and his friend must have seen that he was struggling not to shove deep inside of her and fuck her hard and fast, because he gripped her wrists in his hands, lifted them above her head and pinned them to the mattress. "Let us take care of you, Zara."

"Hurry." She whimpered when Sab's cock moved a little deeper and when he felt the thin membrane of skin guarding her womb his heart and soul filled with emotion and elation. She'd never had sex before and she was theirs. Their mate would never be with any other men other than him and Set.

When her pussy stopped clenching around his hard cock and she began to wiggle he almost lost it, but then he drew in a deep breath and eased his way through the thin membrane and pressed deep until his balls were up against her ass.

"Oh god," Zara groaned and when he saw the moisture in her eyes he felt his heart clench with fear. Fear that he'd hurt her as he'd taken her virginity.

"Are you all right, honey? Did I hurt you?"

"No," she gasped. "Do something! I ache."

"I think our mate wants you to move, Sab," Set whispered and then started kissing her again.

Sab drew his hips back until the head of his cock rested just inside of her entrance and when he slowly surged forward again, he sighed with relief at her moan of pleasure. Although he was holding on to her hips, she managed to bow her pelvis up on another downward stroke, making them both gasp and groan.

Each time he surged forward he pumped his hips faster, sliding his cock in deeper and harder. He panted for breath as he moved, a light sheen of sweat coating his skin. He felt connected to Zara on such a deep emotional level as they made love his heart felt like it was ready to burst wide open.

Set broke the kiss, licking and nibbling at her neck, collar bone and down to her breast again, but Sab needed his friend to move aside because he wanted to feel all of Zara's body under his with their skin connected everywhere. He released her hip, tapped Set on the shoulder, and nodded his head to the side. When Set met his gaze he smiled and then shifted slightly away from Zara. Sab was pleased he and Set were such great friends and didn't need to verbalize every little thing, because he hadn't wanted to distract his mate or divert her attention from him. The moment Set maneuvered aside she had opened her eyes and looked up into his eyes. He hadn't wanted to glance away from her for that brief moment when he met Set's gaze but now that he was once more looking at her, he felt powerful, loved, and needed.

She was looking at him as if he were her entire universe and he knew no one but Zara would ever make him feel that way. He lowered his body over hers. Their skin connected from chest to knees but he made sure to brace his weight on his knees and elbows as he thrust into her hot, tight, wet cunt, faster, deeper. She wrapped her arms around his neck, threading her fingers through his hair and as he leaned down she lifted up. Their lips met in a kiss so wildly passionate he was lost to everything but her.

She moaned and gasped into his mouth and when he felt her internal walls tighten and flutter around his hard dick he knew she was close. He drove in deep as the heat tingling in his lower back spread around to encompass his cock and balls and knew he didn't have long before he shot his load.

He released her lips, kissed and nibbled over her cheek and jaw until he got to her neck and sucked on the sensitive skin beneath her ear before suckling on her earlobe. She mewled as her hips bucked up to meet his, their bodies slapping together and the wet slurping sound of her pussy as she coated his cock with her cream. Her hands moved from his head, down over his shoulders and back. She spread her legs wider, tilting her pelvis up. He sank into her so deep he felt the head of his cock press against the entrance to her womb. He held still, savoring how her pussy walls clenched around his hard length before loosening and clenching again. He panted, drawing breath after breath into his lungs as her tight walls caressed his hard cock, making his dick pulse and twitch with desire and completion.

When she met his gaze again and he saw the intense hunger that mirrored his own, Sab began to move. He withdrew and powered back into her depths. Her eyes fluttered closed, her small, warm delicate hands gripped the cheeks of his ass, and he thrust into her faster, harder, and deeper. A moan of pleasure rumbled in his chest as the smoldering embers began to build back up into a raging inferno, encompassing his lower back and groin. His cock jerked, filling with even more blood, hardening to a point of near blissful pain.

Her cunt rippled around his dick and her lids lifted. Zara's lips parted even more and then her eyes widened and she screamed out her pleasure. Her body quaked and quivered, the muscles in her pussy clenched hard and tight around him as she orgasmed.

Sab pumped his hips faster as the heat and tingles grew more intense and just as he was about to tip over the edge he licked the soft skin at the crook of her neck and shoulder and sank his elongated fangs into her flesh.

Zara cried out as she shot back up into another orgasm. Her body twitched and jerked as juices spilled from her cunt, drenching his cock and balls. Sab drove forward twice more, his shout of completion muffled against her skin as he, too, climaxed. His cock and balls burned as his seed raced up his shaft and erupted from the tip to shoot deep into Zara's body.

He heard and felt a crack as the connection between him and his mate snapped into place. Sab thought the connection he'd felt with her before had been strong but now that he'd claimed Zara as his, he realized that it had been pale in comparison to what he was feeling right now.

Joy like he'd never felt before filled his heart, taking an empty space he hadn't realized he had until he met her and infused him with so much emotion that he felt tears burn the back of his eyes. Love, happiness, completion, and contentment permeated him to his very soul.

His fangs retracted and he licked the mating mark, bathing the wound with his saliva and when he looked at where he'd bitten her, he wasn't really surprised to see the wound was already healing. He perused her gorgeous flushed face and pride filled him when he saw the smile gracing her full lips. Her eyelids fluttered open and his heart stuttered when they filled with tears, but he wasn't worried that he'd hurt her. Now that they were mated he could feel what she was feeling and knew she was as overwhelmed by everything as much as he was.

Her hands lifted from his butt, and although he wanted to tell her to put them back, he didn't. When her arms came up around his neck and she buried her face into his skin, he relished the closeness they shared and felt love surging back and forth between them. If his throat hadn't been so constricted with emotion he would have told her there and then that she was the love of his life, but he was having enough trouble keeping his feelings under control and blinking the tears burning his eyes back. He was content to remain where he was for the rest of his life with his softening cock still buried deep inside of her wet warmth and their bodies pressed against each other's.

If Set hadn't cleared his throat, garnering both of their attention, he may just have stayed like that with Zara forever, but he knew his friend was waiting to claim their mate, too, so with reluctant regret he lifted his head from her sweet smelling skin, kissed her lightly yet reverently on the lips and eased his almost flaccid cock from her body and rolled them both to their sides. Now that he was no longer buried in her he felt a little bereft but if he had his way and Zara was willing he would be making love to her as often as possible.

He finally found the strength to release her and roll from the bed. He so wanted to stay and watch as Set claimed her but decided to give them some privacy. Even though Set had been present as he'd made love to and claimed Zara, his friend hadn't intervened after he'd penetrated her for the first time and it was only fair that he give them the time they needed for the claiming.

With a last glance over his shoulder he left the bedroom and strode into the bathroom. He would take his time cleaning up and hopefully by the time he was done, Set and Zara would be mated. He would fill the tub so they could tend to her afterward and see her settled before he, Set, and the rest of the sentinels struck out in search of the demonic who had managed to escape from the underworld.

Nighttime was when the shadows were at their strongest. If they were to catch the demon who'd taken over the poor soul's body and send the fucker back to the depths of hell to his master, before he could do anymore damage by sacrificing innocent humans to help release his cohorts, they needed to act fast.

He hated the thought of leaving Zara alone but it was their job to protect the innocent and he hoped they could find the shadow demon quickly because he wanted to get back home as fast as possible and hold Zara in his arms as she slept.

He was also scared shitless that one of the demonic in the underworld would find a way through Ra's magical wards and steal her soul as she slept. A released demon couldn't invade dreams once they'd possessed a living body. They only had that ability when they were insubstantial but once they were out amongst the living the fuckers took great pleasure in murdering any living thing they could get their hands on. No man, woman or child would be safe until he and the other sentinels sent the demonic back to the bowels of hell.

* * * *

Zara sighed with satiation and contentedness. She couldn't believe how mating with Sab had given her such a strong connection with him. As she snuggled into Set's embrace she could actually feel Sab's determination to keep the demonic shadows from trying to get to her.

However, that wasn't all she could feel coming from him. She was humbled to feel the deep love he had in his heart and it was all because of her. She'd never thought of herself as anything special but knowing he loved her so much already, after only knowing each other for such a short time, was mind blowing.

She didn't really know how any of this was possible, but now that she'd made up her mind to be Sab's and Set's mate, she didn't regret her decision and wasn't about to question it. Maybe because her men were sentinels to Ra, the sun god, their meeting had been destined in the stars, or should that be the heavens. Or maybe the sun.

She smiled at her own little pun and looked up to see Set watching her intently.

"Are you feeling okay, baby?" Set kissed her shoulder, sending a shiver of arousal racing up her spine.

"Yeah," she sighed and turned over so that she was facing him.

He cupped her cheek, his thumb caressing her skin, sending more tingles of lust through her body, but that wasn't all. She could see emotions in his gaze as well as desire and although she had strong feelings for him, too, she wanted the connection she had with Sab, with Set as well.

"I need you, baby," Set murmured right before his mouth covered hers.

She moaned and gripped his shoulders as he took the kiss deeper. His tongue twirled around in her mouth, along the inside of her cheeks and teeth before coming back to rub against hers. He tasted so good, so right, she could have gone on kissing him for hours. When he released her lips she whimpered with disappointment. She groaned as he licked and nibbled his way down her neck, over her collar bone, and when he got to the pulse point at the bottom of her throat, he paused to suck and lick that spot. Driving her need for him even higher.

She threaded her fingers through his hair when he moved further down her chest and when he laved the tip of his tongue around her areola she gasped, but when he sucked the peak into his mouth she cried out as sparks of lust heated her blood and shot straight down to her cunt.

The edge of his teeth scraped over her nipple before he suckled on it strongly. Zara moved restlessly, her fingers clutching him harder as she tried to bring him closer, but Set wouldn't be swayed. He shifted his mouth to her other breast and suckled on the peak for what seemed like hours, but was surely only minutes.

When he lifted his head she met his hungry gaze and her breath stuttered in her throat. He was so damn handsome and sexy, he took her breath away.

Set maneuvered onto his knees, gently pushing her from her side to her back and then he crawled up over her. When he was in the position he wanted to be, straddling her lower thighs and knees, he skimmed his hands up the inside of her legs, spreading them further apart. She sighed with pleasure when he reached her pussy lips but instead of stroking them like she expected, he tugged on them gently, sending zings of bliss into her cunt. Her internal muscles clenched and cream dripped from her body. She'd never thought having her labia pulled would turn her on so much but the more he did it, the hornier she got.

"Please, Set?"

"Do you want my cock in your pussy, baby?" He gave her a wicked smile before looking down at her pussy again.

"Oh god," she gasped when he rimmed a finger around her wet hole and then slowly pressed it up inside of her. He withdrew it and then shoved back in. Zara spread her legs wider and drew them up against her body, giving him unimpeded access to her hungry pussy.

Having his finger sliding in and out of her sheath was heavenly but she wanted his cock filling her up, gliding in and out of her wet cunt until she screamed.

She hadn't even noticed that she'd closed her eyes until Set's finger stopped moving and she lifted her lids. With their gazes locked he shifted, placing his hands on the mattress near her shoulders and then he lowered his body over hers.

His groan joined her moan as their bodies met. The heat emanating off of him was incredible and when she lowered her gaze to his mouth and she saw his fangs, her heart skipped a beat. When she'd first seen those elongated teeth she'd been frightened but not this time, because when Sab had sunk those sharp puppies into her skin she screamed with euphoria. Now she knew what to expect she was eager to experience Set sinking those sharp puppies into her shoulder and making her scream.

Zara had no idea what Set was waiting for but she needed him inside of her now, so she reached up, placed her hand on his nape, and pulled his mouth to hers. She didn't worry about him cutting her or drawing blood with those teeth because she didn't care. All that mattered was that he fill her wet, hungry pussy and claim her.

He must have felt the same way because he shifted his hips and when the head of his cock brushed against her clit she moaned into his mouth. He moved again, the tip of his dick lowering until he was against her entrance and then he pushed in.

Zara broke the kiss and gasped for air as she released her hold on the back of his neck and caressed her hands over his shoulders, arms, and sides until she got to his hips. Once more they locked gazes as he slowly worked his thick, hard cock into her soaked pussy.

If she thought it would work Zara would have pressed up into his slow strokes but she could see by the look of determination in his eyes that he wanted to protract their time together.

He moved his weight to his elbows and then cupped her breasts, kneading and molding the globes before pinching the nipples between his fingers and thumbs. By the time he was fully embedded into her cunt she felt as if her whole body was on fire.

A sob of frustration or maybe it was famishment left her mouth when he released her breasts but then she moaned when he pressed his chest to hers. His mouth descended on hers and as he began to kiss her rapaciously, he began to rock his hips.

Zara's hands moved to his ass and she dug her fingers into the muscular cheeks as she began to move her hips with his. Each time he drove down into her cunt deeply, she pushed her pelvis up to meet his strokes. Liquid lava flowed through her veins, heating her body from within and each time his cock glided along her walls creating that delicious friction, the tension began to build. She moaned when he lifted his mouth from hers and started licking and nibbling on her neck.

When he scraped those sharp teeth on the sensitive spot just beneath her ear, Zara was lost. Lost to everything but Set. She was surrounded by his musky, manly scent, savored each and every touch and the pressure building inside each time he pumped his hips, gliding his cock in and out of her wet cunt. Her internal walls closed in around his shuttling dick, her pussy getting tighter and tighter around his thick girth, making them both moan.

He rocked his hips faster, deeper, harder each time the bulbous broad head of his erection caressed that sensitive internal spot on the top wall of her cunt, making her writhe and moan as she raced toward ecstasy.

Zara screamed as she began coming. Set gasped and groaned as he drove his hard cock in her faster, if that was even possible and just as the contractions in her cunt began to slow, he sank his fangs into her neck and shoulder. Her mouth opened on a soundless cry, her body shaking and quaking, juices dripping from her pussy and bright lights formed before her eyes.

Set roared against her neck, the sound muffled on her skin as he ground his groin into hers, his cock going deeper than ever before.

His cock seemed to expand inside of her, prolonging her climax and spurts of heat filled her channel and womb. The orgasm seemed to last for a nirvanic lifetime and yet it was over before she was anywhere near ready for it to be.

When her soul finally floated back into her body she felt the connection with Set and before she knew it, tears welled in her eyes and spilled down over her temples into her hair.

Set had already pulled his fangs out of her flesh and was licking at the spot where he'd bitten her. She was surrounded by him, his softening cock was still buried deep inside of her, but it was the emotions in her heart that had her crying. Now that he and Sab had claimed her as their mate she could feel them both in her heart and soul.

The love she could feel from them for her was astoundingly humbling and she couldn't contain the feelings building inside of her for a moment longer. The sob erupted from deep inside of her chest and out of her parted lips before she could stop it and another followed quickly behind.

Set's body tensed as he shoved an arm beneath her shoulders and then he rolled until he was lying upon the mattress on his back with her body draped over him. His hands moved from her shoulders down her back and ass before making the return journey as she cried.

Zara had never been so happy in her life and hoped like hell that the demonic shadows her mates had told her about didn't find a way to get to her or her guys. Fierce possessiveness surged through her body and entrenched into her heart and she knew that if at all possible she would do anything and everything she could to keep them safe. Even if it meant breathing her last breath for them so that they could continue to live.

Chapter Nine

Apep looked around the cavern from his seat on the raised throne with a bored expression on his face, but he was anything but. The attempt to poison the female two of Ra's sentinels were enamored with had failed and heads were about to roll. He should have known that Sturgis would fuck things up. He was one of his strongest demons and although he'd been given instructions to follow and as far as he knew had done so, the plan hadn't worked.

The fucking sun god had been the bane of his existence. If it weren't for him he would have had control of the world thousands of years ago. Ra had stuck his nose in where it wasn't wanted and they'd been enemies ever since. Apep had controlled the Egyptian pharaohs, directing them to steal, torture, and create. Those pyramids had been created because of him. He'd had no idea the sun god had been watching him as he directed the weak, greedy humans.

Anger coursed through him, causing his dark power to surge out, burning his idiot followers. Their cries of fear and agony were balms to his black soul and made him laugh. He slumped on his throne, squeezed his fists, and watched the shadows writhing in agony.

Ra had somehow contained his powers to the underworld and although he wanted to make his minions human, he couldn't. It had taken him almost a thousand years to figure out that sending his shadows to the earth above and having them steal souls from the innocent while they slept was the only way for them to be able to walk amongst the humans.

The only way Ra could have become so powerful was if he had gone to Amun. That slimy fucker had thought he was the ruler of all the Egyptian gods but Apep had known better. He was supposed to have ruled the heavens and earth. The only way Ra could have become more powerful than him was if those two bastards had somehow combined their powers.

Fury turned his gaze red as he thought about the day Ra had intervened and saved the Egyptian slaves. He laughed maliciously as his demons screamed in agony, imaging it was Ra instead. He'd been minding his own damned business and watching the scene below him with malevolent humor, but then he'd felt the power racing over his skin and when he'd tried to turn to face his nemesis, he hadn't been able to.

"You aren't worthy of the title god," Amun's voice was so loud he'd felt his eardrums burst and he'd bled for the first time since he'd become a god. The warm fluid had leaked from his ears, over his jaw and down his neck. For that alone he'd vowed to kill Amun.

Ra had appeared in front of him and the anger in his gaze had been palpable but he underestimated the god and hadn't considered him a threat. He hadn't understood what was happening when Ra had jerked and then his skin had begun to glow but before he could even think about the anomaly he'd been thrust into the bowels of hell.

He remembered screaming at the searing pain as fire had scorched the skin from his body and he'd tried to run. That had only made him want vengeance with a passion. He'd never felt such pain or felt so cowardly, but he was strong and powerful and he'd learned to stop fighting the burning agony and had embraced it. It had taken hundreds of years for his powers to strengthen and when it had, he'd taken on Hades and won. Now he was the leader of the underworld and the evil spirits were his to control, to dictate to, or to kill.

What he wouldn't tolerate was failure. Any shadow that failed him would die a painful death over and over again.

He sighed as the fury began to lower to a slow simmer. It was getting harder and harder to find humans pure and innocent enough to steal souls from. If he'd been able to touch the children he would have won his war with the sun god long ago, but they were the purest of all the humans and were protected by the hand of God himself. If his minions even touched on the edge of a child's soul, he'd disintegrate into dust and die, never to return.

He'd learnt by trial and error what worked and what didn't but humanity had advanced in leaps and bounds over the last couple of centuries and with that advancement came knowledge, corruption, greed, and selfishness.

Apep rubbed at his forehead as a thought popped into his head. He wondered if stealing the souls of evil humans would enhance his minions' power enough to coalesce into a solid form. He'd tried that three thousand years ago but it hadn't worked. The evil ones had been able to circumvent his dictates and think for themselves. They'd caused a lot of destruction and deaths of the innocent people he was trying to find, but maybe things had changed enough that he would be able to control them in totality.

His powers had grown stronger and stronger so maybe he could use those not so worthy humans after all.

* * * *

Zara had no idea how long she slept but when consciousness returned she felt happy, content, and well loved. She felt Sab's and Set's bodies pressed up against hers and she sighed with bliss. Last night had been extraordinarily, blissfully carnal and if she had her way she would spend the rest of her life loving her two mates.

As she came more awake she felt the connection humming between the three of them, but that wasn't all she felt. Zara felt healthier than she'd ever been in her life, stronger and her senses were sharper. She could smell Set's sandalwood scent as well as Sab's spicy, cinnamon tang mixed in with their natural male musk.

Sab moved behind her and she moaned when his hand gripped one of her ass cheeks and kneaded the globe. She opened her eyes when

Set moved in front of her and her breath caught in her throat when she saw the love in his gaze. She smiled softly at him and his lips lifted in response.

"How are you feeling, baby?" Set asked, his voice a little gravelly from sleep.

"Wonderful."

"You certainly do," Sab whispered before kissing her bare shoulder.

"I can feel you both. It's..."

"You don't have to explain it to us, honey." Sab smoothed his hand over her ass, hip, and then up her stomach to her breast.

She sighed with pleasure when his hand enveloped her breast, molding its shape before he plucked at her nipple. Her eyes lowered as they began to close but she opened them again when Set cupped her cheek, jaw, and neck in the large palm of his hand. His hand was so big his fingers were halfway down her neck, but she loved the sensation of his touch on her sensitive skin. In fact she loved both of them touching her.

"We can feel you in our hearts and souls." Set kissed her softly on the lips.

Zara nearly groaned with frustration when he pulled away again, but they gently pushed her to her back. Sab turned her face toward him and ran a hand over her body, stopping to rub and knead in strategic places as he kissed her.

She felt the mattress dip when Set shifted down the bed and when his hands landed on her knees and gently parted her thighs she groaned as the ambient air in the room caressed over her wet, heated folds. She didn't know which one of her mates had pushed the covers down nor when, but she didn't really care. All she cared about was having both of them loving her again. The orgasms they gave her the previous night were carnally consummate to the self-induced ones she'd given herself upon occasion and she was eager to experience that their touch again.

She tensed for a moment when she felt Set's hot breath against her cunt but with the first swipe of his tongue over her wet pussy, she relaxed and moaned with bliss. How could anything so carnally erotic give so much pleasure?

"You taste sweeter than honey, baby," Set said in a raspy voice before he lowered his head again.

Zara gasped in air when Sab released her mouth and groaned when he kissed down to her chest. His tongue swirled around her areola and then he sucked the hard tipped nipple into his hot, wet mouth. She shifted on the mattress restlessly as her mates sent her up toward the stars.

Liquid heat raced through her body and although she felt totally boneless the tension began to build. A soft cry left her lips when Set pressed two fingers into her cunt, thrusting them in and out of her pussy, creating that amazingly delectable friction which sent her climbing the slope faster. Copious amounts of cream dripped from her pussy and her internal muscles rippled and coiled.

Set's tongue flicked over her clit, sending shards of pleasure deep into her womb and just as she thought she was about to fall over the edge, Set pressed a finger onto her anus. This time she tensed for an entirely different reason. She wasn't sure what to make of the astounding pleasure of having Set's finger caress over her ass.

"Do you like that, baby?"

"I–I…don't…know."

"What's he doing to you, honey?" Sab asked after releasing her nipple from his mouth.

"He's…he's…"

"Is Set playing with your ass?" Sab held her gaze, lowered his head, and swiped his tongue over her nipple.

"Oh god," Zara moaned and arched her chest up toward him. All of a sudden she felt like she was on fire for them. She wanted to lift her legs up and spread her knees wide so that her mates had access to both her holes. She didn't even realize she was shaking until Set pulled his fingers from her body and sat up between her knees.

Sab sat up as well, lifted her from the bed with ease, and placed her in his lap. She buried her face in his neck and tried to stop trembling but the harder she tried the more her body quaked. When her teeth began to chatter and the heat invading her body began to burn her insides she began to get scared. Had the demonic somehow infiltrated her mates' hideout and gotten to her? Had they stolen a piece of her soul and doomed her to a painful death?

"Shit! What's going on?" Sab asked.

"I think it's the bond." Set sat behind her and pressed his back to her front.

"I don't feel very well," Zara said through her chattering teeth.

"Wrap her up," Sab ordered. "We need to get her to Ra's temple."

Zara had felt wonderful when she'd awoken but now she could barely keep her eyes open. She felt hot on the outside but her insides felt like they were slowly freezing. The combination of the hot and cold was sapping every ounce of her energy and although she tried to lift an arm to brush the hair away from her face she could barely manage to move a finger. When she swallowed her throat felt dry and raw, a bit like when she had tonsillitis as a kid and felt as if she was trying to swallow glass.

She murmured a protest when Set wrapped her up in a robe, but when he took hold of her wrist to put her arms in the sleeves she cried out in agony. Her skin was so sensitive having them touch her was painful.

"Stop," Sab yelled. "You're hurting her."

"Not on purpose," Set yelled back. "I stopped as soon as I felt her pain."

"Yeah, I know. Sorry." Sab's voice sounded like it was a long way off.

"Just make sure she's covered so the others don't see her. We need to get her to Ra."

Zara had to strain to hear Set's last words because they sounded so quiet. The only thing she could hear now was her blood racing through her veins and the loud rapid beat of her own heart. She didn't want to die after just finding Set and Sab but she had no strength to fight whatever was happening to her and she wasn't sure she would survive it.

* * * *

"En!" Set roared as he and Sab rushed toward Ra's temple. He'd never been so fucking scared in his life. He had no idea what was wrong with Zara and he felt so damn useless. What good was all the powers he had when he couldn't even help his mate?

Sab stopped under the triangular glass pyramid and sank to his knees. Set knelt at his friend's side and between them they carefully arranged Zara into a more comfortable position and then tugged at the robe Set had wrapped around her naked body.

"What's going on?" En asked as he entered the room.

"Something's wrong with Zara. She's sick." Set's voice cracked on the last word and he had to clear his throat and take a deep steadying breath.

"Did you call Ra?" Pen asked.

Set looked beyond En to see that the rest of the sentinels had entered the temple. They were all frowning with concern and he had no doubt he looked the same as them if not more worried.

"Tell me what happened." En squatted next to Zara and felt her pulse.

Sab started to explain what they'd done that morning and how their mate had gone from being well to sick in the blink of an eye.

En brushed the hair back from Zara's face and nape and then turned to look at Set before meeting Sab's eyes. "You claimed her." The wonder in En's voice had Set shifting uncomfortably.

"Yes," he responded. "She agreed."

"Hey." En held a hand up at Set's belligerent tone. "I didn't think you'd forced her, mated her without her permission. I just needed to confirm so I can figure out what's wrong with her."

"And can you?" Sab asked.

"Her pulse is a little fast as is her respiration and she feels like she has a fever."

"You think she's come down with something?" Mit asked as he moved closer.

"That would be my guess if these two hadn't claimed her, but since they have she shouldn't be susceptible to human diseases or illnesses."

"So what do you think is wrong?" Pen asked.

"Could her body be going through a change?" Menna crouched down beside them, staring at Zara's face.

Set glanced up when he felt a surge of power sweep the room, making the hair on his arms and neck stand on end. Ra appeared out of nowhere, nodded to the other sentinels who moved aside at the sun god's approach. Sab was now holding Zara's hand and Set knew by the determined look in his eyes that he wasn't about to shift away from their mate.

Ra didn't say a word but he crouched down and placed his hand on Zara's forehead and another on her robe-covered stomach. He closed his eyes and began to speak but whatever he said wasn't audible to anyone but him.

Set held his breath when the god's hands began to glow and the aura of gold spread out to encompass the whole of Zara's body. When Ra opened his eyes he met Sab's and then Set's gazes.

"Your mate will be fine. She was going through the change. I've sped up the process, and it's now done."

"What does that mean?" Set asked angrily. He was pissed off that their woman had been suffering and he had a feeling Ra had left out pertinent information.

"She is now immortal and with each year that passes her strength and senses will grow until she is as strong as the both of you are."

"Did you know this would happen?" Sab asked in a quiet yet hard voice.

Set had never heard that tone of voice from his friend when he'd had dealings with the sun god, but he understood his angst just fine.

"Don't you remember the change?" Ra looked at them and then at the other sentinels. "You all experienced the same reaction."

"Not really," Set replied and sighed with frustration. He didn't care about remembering his own transformation to a demigod. It had been so fucking long since that had happened. What he cared about was the here and now. About Zara.

Ra just shrugged his shoulders in a very human gesture and then disappeared. The others turned and began leaving the room. Just as Set lifted Zara into his arms she sighed and shifted. The robe he'd wrapped her in slipped and his heart stuttered, his breath caught in his throat when the material slipped, and he caught sight of a dark mark on the top of her left breast.

He pushed the robe aside and he stopped breathing altogether when he saw the mark of Ra's eye outlined on her beautiful creamy skin.

"Fuck! That's sexy," Mit said.

Set lifted his gaze from Zara's chest, pulling the material back over to cover her and glared at the other sentinel.

Mit held his hands up palms out and chuckled. "Hey, I didn't mean anything by it. Just saying…" He didn't finish his sentence but spun on his heel and hurried from the temple, his laughter echoing down the corridor.

"Let's get her back to our rooms." Sab brushed a hand over her hair and led the way out.

Set had just placed her on the bed when she sighed again and rolled to her side. The robe slipped from her body, exposing the upper half of her sexy form.

That was when he saw the falcon etched on her left shoulder blade. The detail of the mark was amazing. It looked like a tattoo but he knew it wasn't. The outline was black but the delicately etched feathers were a brown color with small streaks of white mixed in. However that wasn't the only mark on her back. On her right shoulder blade was a smaller version of Ra's eye which formed the eye of another falcon. He wondered what the significance was and then thought maybe it was because they had mated her and that was a sign of her joining.

"Check this out," Set glanced at Sab and then back to Zara's back.

Sab skirted the bed and then knelt next to him. "That's amazing. I wonder why she has three marks on her."

"Maybe because she's our mate," Set suggested.

Sab nodded. "Could be." He leaned closer and then his finger traced a very thin white line that Set hadn't seen.

Set gasped when he saw what the faint outline was. The border was almost the same color of her skin but now that Sab had pointed it out he could see that it was in the shape of what he thought an angel would look like. The image was nearly an exact copy of Zara but with angel wings.

"That is amazing," Set whispered with awe.

"Yeah." Sab nodded.

"What's going on?" Zara asked as she rolled to her back and then gasped as she covered her bare breasts with her arm.

Chapter Ten

Her face flamed when she realized she was practically naked. She wasn't used to having a man or men looking at her nakedness and felt a little shy. She frowned because she remembered that they were both kissing and touching her and then she began to feel hot and cold at the same time and sick to her stomach. Everything after that was a blank.

She noticed the robe covering her lower half and reached for it, yanking it up to cover her breasts.

"Look at your chest, baby." Set reached out and stroked a finger over the skin on her chest. She looked down but didn't see anything so she gave him a raised eyebrow in query.

Sab gripped the robe and tugged it down. Zara's heart began to race when she saw the same tattoo on the upper slope of her left breast. Her breath hitched and she lifted her hand to trace the outline with her finger. She'd thought it was a tattoo but now she wasn't so sure. Her skin wasn't sore like it should be if she'd just had a tattoo artist ink her skin with a needle. In fact her flesh didn't look or feel as if anything had dug into it.

"You have three marks on your back," Sab said in a quiet voice.

Zara got up onto her hands and knees and started crawling down the bed. The robe got caught beneath one of her knees and slid from her body. Two low masculine groans sounded and she looked back over her shoulder to see that Sab and Set were both staring at her ass. She smiled and when she saw hunger in their eyes her body responded. If she didn't want to see the marks on her back so bad, she would have turned back around and begged them to make love to her.

She gained her feet and stumbled but caught her balance quickly. As she walked toward the bathroom she mulled over how strong and healthy she felt. In fact she felt downright invigorated.

Zara flipped on the light switch, moved closer to the vanity and the mirror on the wall above it, then turned so her back was facing toward the mirror. She gasped when she saw the marks on her shoulder blades. When she caught movement in the mirror she looked up to see that Set and Sab had entered the room and were watching her.

"What do they mean?"

Set and Sab both walked toward her and stood on either side of her. She turned to face them.

"We think that now you're like us, Ra marked you as one of his." Sab clasped one of her hands in his and Set took the other.

"What?" She frowned.

"You got real sick when you went through the transformation," Set said in a growly voice.

"We took you to Ra's temple because we were scared you were dying." Sab squeezed her hand and when she met his gaze she could see lingering fear in his eyes.

"What transformation?" she asked. Her heart stopped for a beat and then began pounding hard against her sternum.

"When we mated and bit you, apparently it started a transformation. You are now immortal like we are," Set explained.

"Did you know that would happen?" Zara asked. If they had and hadn't told her she was going to give them a piece of her mind. They should have told her what to expect before they had claimed her.

Sab shook his head. "We had no idea, but according to Ra we went through the same thing when we became sentinels."

"So am I a sentinel now, too?"

"In a way, I guess you are, but there is no way in hell we want you fighting," Sab stated in a firm voice.

"Why not?"

Set and Sab both released her hands. Sab stood before her, staring at her with a frown on his face. Set turned away, took a few steps, and then turned back.

"There is no fucking way we are going to allow you to put yourself in danger."

Zara glared at Set. She didn't like to be dictated to and wasn't about to let him get away with doing so.

"You don't have any say in what I do." She moved closer and poked him in the chest.

"Yes I, we do. You're our mate, Zara. I'll tie you to that fucking bed if that's what it takes to keep you safe." Set's gaze was full of determination.

Anger surged through Zara, making her body shake. She licked her lips and then froze when she felt what she thought were two of her teeth lengthening. She spun back around to look in the mirror and stared at herself in fascinated horror. She had fangs.

Her eye teeth were quite a bit longer than they should have been and the tips looked like they were razor sharp.

"What the fuck is happening to me?" When she heard herself lisp, tears formed in her eyes and she covered her mouth with her hand.

Sab released her hand, pulled her into his arms and up against his body. "Don't panic, honey. You're still the same person you were before, just a little more."

"Does this mean I have to drink blood?" she asked and mentally cursed when her voice quavered.

"Not if you don't want to, baby." Set stroked a hand over her head.

Zara sighed. She wasn't sure what to make of any of this, but there was one thing she was certain of. She wasn't about to let Sab and Set tell her what to do. Maybe she could talk them into training her how to fight and when they went out to protect humanity she could help them.

"Good," she said and rested her head on Sab's chest. The heat of his body seeped into her and she began to get aroused, but first she needed to make sure that they knew she wasn't going to put up with any of their shit. She didn't care that they were thousands of years older than she was, or that they were demigods. She was an independent woman and she wasn't about to let them take over her life. It was bad enough that she was in hiding because of those shadow demons. Now that she'd been changed and was immortal she wanted to help find those assholes and take them down.

I'm immortal. Excitement surged through her body. She wouldn't grow old and die. Nor would she ever get another cold, flu or any other human disease. She wanted to laugh with joy but she needed to get her mind back on to what was important.

Those dreams she'd had of her soul being tugged on as the demonic had tried to steal it from her had been terrifying and it had hurt like hell but she wasn't going to sit back like a damsel in distress and let them take control. She was so far from that analogy it was almost laughable.

She looked up at Sab and then Set. "You aren't going to be with me twenty four hours a day, seven days a week. I want to learn what I need to in order to help you fight these demons."

"No," Set immediately replied emphatically.

"Don't take that tone with me." Zara scowled at him. "What the hell am I supposed to do if you aren't here and the demons find me?"

"She's right," Sab said quietly.

Set turned to glare at Sab. "No she's fucking not."

Zara clenched her teeth and almost yelped. Her fangs pierced her lower lip, drawing blood, but she ignored the pain and embraced the ire. "Yes, I damn well am." She shoved Set in the chest and then covered her mouth in horror as he went flying through the air, landed on the bed before tumbling over it and landed with a thud on the floor. "Oh. My. God."

She skirted around Sab and hurried over to Set. He was lying on the floor with a shocked dazed expression on his face. She knelt down next to him and clutched his hand. "Are you all right? God, I am so sorry. I had no idea I could do that."

"That was fucking amazing." Sab laughed as he came toward her and tugged her to her feet. He lifted her against his chest, spun around in a circle and laughed.

"Holy shit!" Set pushed to his feet and shook his head as if to clear it.

"Do you agree with her now?" Sab asked as he grinned at Set.

Set nodded and then swallowed. "Yeah, we'll start first thing in the morning."

"The guys aren't going to believe this." Sab chuckled.

Set smiled. "Maybe we can have a little fun."

Zara was aware of what they were saying but the moment Sab had lifted her into his arms she became aroused. Her bare breasts were pressed against his chest and every time he moved his muscles flexed and her nipples hardened. Juices coated her folds and dripped out onto her thighs.

Set pressed his chest against her back and kissed her shoulder, making her shiver.

When Zara gazed up at Sab she saw he wasn't looking at her but over the top of her head at Set. With each breath she took her body heated even more and when her empty cunt clenched and she leaked more cream she decided to take matters into her own hands.

She hooked her arms around Sab's neck, threaded her fingers into his hair, and tugged his head down as she wrapped her legs around his waist. She moaned when her hot, wet, needy pussy came into contact with his jeans-covered dick and then she pressed her mouth to his.

He opened his mouth and let her take the lead. She licked into his mouth, tasting his amazingly delectable flavor on her tongue and savored it.

"She needs us," Set said before he sucked on the sensitive skin beneath her ear.

Zara whimpered when his hands landed on her hips and then skimmed and caressed their way up her sides before moving back down to her ass. He squeezed her cheeks and then he pulled them apart.

Zara groaned with frustration when Sab broke the kiss and lowered her feet onto the floor. "Don't worry, honey. We'll take care of you."

Set let her butt go and then turned her around to face him. As he lowered his head she stood up on her toes to meet him halfway. He cupped her face between his hands and slanted his mouth over hers.

Zara was so hot for both of them she actually climbed up his body, wrapping her arms and legs around his neck and waist. She lost herself in his kiss. In the desire coursing through her veins and his skin up against hers. She registered that Set was moving but didn't care where he was taking her. All she cared about was having the fire burning inside of her extinguished.

A sigh left her mouth when her back connected with something soft and Set moved away from her. When she saw that Sab had entered the room and he stopped when he was standing next to Set she wondered what was going on. Didn't they want her now that she'd mated with them? She mentally shook her head. No, she could feel their desire for her through the amazing connection she had. It was faint but it was there.

She wondered how strong she would be able to feel them and them her once the connections strengthened. She had no idea how she knew it would get stronger, maybe it was instinct, and although she was a little wary about feeling what they did and they would feel what she did, she wasn't scared of it. She was nervous about the fangs and the changes she'd apparently gone through but she would worry about that later. Right now she needed her men to love her.

Both Sab and Set tugged at the buttons on their pants, pushed them over their hips and down their legs before kicking them away. She licked her dry lips when she spied their erect cocks. They were so freaking big and if she hadn't already had them inside of her she would have been as nervous as hell.

Set walked around the end of the bed and pulled out the drawer in the bedside table. Zara was curious about what he was after but her curiosity waned when Sab crawled up onto the bed and kneeled over her, his hands beside her head. He bent his elbows and kissed her on the lips.

Zara gasped as his tongue stroked into hers and reached up to caress her hands over his delectable hard chest and ridged stomach. He groaned into her mouth just before he released her lips, licking and nibbling his way down to her breasts. The moment his mouth closed over one stiff peak she cried out, gripping his arms and trying to tug him down on top of her. She needed him or Set to fill her hungry cunt before she went insane.

She bowed her chest up, pushing more of her breast into his mouth and he didn't disappoint her. He sucked as much of her in as he could and suckled strongly. She felt the blood in her breast rising to the surface of her skin and wondered if he would leave a mark on her. She hoped so. She couldn't think of anything sexier than having love bites on her skin as a reminder of her mates loving her.

Sab drew up with his mouth until only her nipple was in his moist cavern and she whimpered when he flicked his tongue over the sensitive nub before scraping his teeth over it.

He released her breast and then he lowered down until his body was pressed all along hers, wrapped his arms around her shoulders, and started kissing her mouth voraciously. Each tongue swirl and lick made her body throb with desire until she was almost sobbing with each inhale and exhalation.

Sab's muscles tensed and then he rolled so that he was on the mattress with her on top of him. His legs were inside of hers and her pelvis was aligned with his. He spread his legs wider, splaying hers further apart and she realized why when she felt Set's breath on the back of her neck.

Set licked and sucked on her neck, shoulder and then he moved and licked where the tattoo-type marks were. The moment his tongue touched the falcon on her left shoulder blade her pussy clenched and cream wept from her cunt.

Sab broke the kiss and glanced up at Set. "Whatever you're doing, keep it up. She just creamed herself."

"I'm licking one of her marks."

"Is that so?" Sab met her gaze, gave her a wicked grin and then leaned up and swirled his tongue around the eye of Ra mark on the top of her left breast.

Zara shivered and gasped. Her internal walls clamped around nothing and she growled with frustration. Everything they did to her felt absolutely divine but she needed to have them inside her taking the emptiness away.

"Please," she gasped when Sab sucked on the mark.

"What do you want, baby?" Set asked before he moved his mouth to the other mark on her right shoulder blade.

"I want you. Both of you. Inside of me. Now!" Zara didn't care that she came across as demanding. She needed her mates to relieve the aching hunger in her womb and deep in her soul.

Set pressed a hand on her back between her shoulder blades and Zara lowered her body until her breasts were squished against Sab's chest. She jolted when he placed a cool moist finger against her anus and then moaned when he circled that finger around and around her star. She'd never even realized how sensitive her ass was until now, and although she was a little trepidatious about what was about to happen, she also wanted it. Needed it. Zara needed to have both her ass and cunt filled with cock and hopefully her mates would be able to quench the fiery hunger burning through her body.

She gasped when Set's thick, manly, lubed finger breached her anus and held her breath as he pushed that digit deeper. There wasn't any pain, which surprised her because she'd heard having anal sex could hurt, but Set was being really gentle with her and since they were sort of connected, maybe he could feel what she did. If that was the case then she considered it a plus right now, because she knew he wouldn't do anything to hurt her.

"Does that feel good, honey?" Sab asked as he tugged on her hair to get her attention.

Zara lifted her head from his shoulder and met his gaze. She moaned, licked her dry lips, and then nodded. "So good."

Sab's gaze turned hotter just before he took her face between his palms, angled her head to his liking, and then his mouth was on hers.

Zara sighed and kissed him back with all the hunger racing through her veins. Their tongues danced and twirled around each other's before rubbing together. She was so turned on by his and Set's tastes, their touches and the connection they had she couldn't get enough. When the opportunity arose she wrapped her lips around the tip of his tongue and sucked it into her mouth. The low growly sound he made low in his throat vibrated his chest and her nipples became even harder.

Her anus began to stretch a little more and she realized that Set was pressing another finger up into her back entrance. She broke the kiss with Sab and panted for air and tried to wiggle her hips. A sharp slap landed on her butt cheek, causing her pussy to release more juices as it clenched.

"She likes having her ass smacked," Sab rasped. "Her juices are all over my cock and I'm not even inside of her yet."

"We'll have to explore that later," Set said in a growly voice as he added another finger to her ass.

Zara moaned as her muscles stretched to accommodate his pumping and scissoring digits. She felt so full, yet empty at the same time. She sobbed in protest when he removed his fingers from her star but then Sab clasped her hips and lifted her up to her knees.

"Take me inside you, mate." He kept their gazes locked as she took the base of his cock in her hand and held it up straight.

Zara lowered her body and whimpered when the head of his dick penetrated her pussy. Her muscles clamped around the tip as if to draw him in deeper before loosening again.

"So fucking tight and wet," Sab panted, his fingers flexing on her hips as if trying to stop himself from tugging her all the way down over his cock.

The muscles in Zara's thighs clenched and she gripped his biceps as she began to move up and down his hard dick, taking more and more of him into her until her ass cheeks were resting on her thighs.

"Fuck yeah," Sab rasped as he lifted her up and pulled her down harder.

Zara moaned at the sensational pleasure of having his cock sliding in and out of her cunt, caressing her internal walls. He continued to thrust his hips up faster, harder, and deeper until her ass was slapping against his body. She was quickly climbing the slope to nirvana but she didn't want to go over without Set.

Set must have been of the same mind because he pushed against her shoulder and she leaned lower over Sab without any hesitation. She was so famished for her mates she was trembling. Her pussy and ass wouldn't stop pulsing.

"Relax for me, baby." Set whispered against her ear, causing a shiver of desire to race up her spine, but when he swirled and laved his tongue over the falcon mark on her left shoulder she cried out. It felt so damn good she wasn't sure she would survive it, but she didn't care. She just wanted both of her mates filling her up and taking away the ache deep inside.

Set kept his arm around her waist and then he gripped her shoulder with his hand. She groaned when the head of his hard dick pressed against her star and dug her nails into Sab's skin.

"Take a deep breath for me, Zara," Set directed in a breathless voice. "As I push in, I want you to push out."

Zara swallowed and nodded, words beyond her capability right then, but she did as Set told her. The skin around her anus burned slightly as Set penetrated her back hole but it wasn't enough to make her want him to stop. In fact, the total opposite. That pinching feeling made her hungrier to have her rosette filled.

"Fucking hell," Set growled as he began to gently rock his hips, sliding his cock in and out but going a little deeper each time he moved forward.

"What?" Sab asked through clenched teeth.

Zara saw that he was as worked up as she was. There were beads of sweat on his forehead, the muscles and tendons in his neck stood up beneath his skin, and he was breathing heavily.

"She has the tightest, sexiest ass."

Zara would have laughed but Set pushed in the last bit, sending streaks of desire deep into her ass, cunt and womb. She had no idea that having both of her holes filled at the same time would be so carnally good and she couldn't wait to have them both moving inside of her.

"Move!" she demanded, her voice coming out more guttural than she'd ever heard from herself before.

"Let's give our mate what she wants," Sab rasped.

Set drew his dick back out of her ass until just the tip remained inside and as he pressed back in Sab withdrew from her cunt.

Zara whimpered with need and bliss as her mates began to love her. Each time they drove into her holes they increased the speed of their pumping hips until they were counter thrusting in a rhythm that had her racing toward the peak.

Liquid heat pooled low in her belly and she began to move with Set and Sab. She undulated her hips, forward and back, up and down, taking and giving pleasure, hoping her mates would climax with her.

The inner walls of her cunt began to coil, the friction of having their cocks sliding in and out of her star and pussy, building the tension to unbelievable heights. Her legs were trembling, as was the rest of her, but she wasn't about to stop. She needed to come so bad and she wanted their seed filling her up.

"I'm close," Set groaned as he drove his cock deep into her ass before pulling back again.

"Me too," Sab gasped. "Let go, honey."

Zara gasped when Sab pressed a finger to her engorged clit and then she moaned when he began to rub the sensitive bundle of nerves. Her body grew so taut she wondered if it would snap but then she wasn't thinking at all.

She screamed as the orgasm hit her like a tsunami hit the shore. Wave after wave of rapture washed over her, sending her spiralling up into the heavens of nirvana. Her whole body shook and shivered, her internal muscles clamped and released, and cream dripped from her cunt as Sab and Set continued to shuttle their cocks in and out of her anus and cunt.

Fangs exploded from her gums and she had the wildest urge to bite both Sab and Set. She was so lost in bliss she didn't even think about what she was doing.

Zara leaned down, licked the crook of Sab's shoulder and neck, and sank her fangs into his flesh. The sweet taste of his blood coated her tongue and she drank his life essence down.

Sab roared as he shoved his cock deep into her pussy. Zara felt him twitching and expanding inside of her and the heat of his ejaculation as he filled her with his cum.

Set pressed his front to her back, licked the mating mark he'd previously made, and sank his fangs in deep. Zara's cry of joy as she was sent over into another orgasm was muffled against Sab's skin. Her teeth retracted and she bathed the wound site with her tongue and then she turned her head toward Set. He'd just removed his teeth from her neck and after licking the bite he leaned toward her more.

Zara nuzzled his neck with her nose, breathed in his wonderful manly scent and bit down.

Set shouted as he stroked his cock as deep as it would go into her ass and came. His dick jerked and juddered each time he spumed his cum deep into her body. Zara moaned at the different taste of his blood but savored each little sip as she swallowed it down.

When her fangs receded she licked the wound clean and flopped down against Sab's chest. She was so satiated she felt like a wet dishrag but she also felt a little drunk. That was until Sab tilted her neck slightly, brushed her hair out of the way, and sank his elongated teeth into her.

Lightning streaks flashed across her eyes as she once more shot into the stratosphere. Her body quaked and quivered, her internal muscles contracted as juices gushed from her pussy.

Emotions poured through the link from Sab and Set, filling her heart and soul with so much love she couldn't contain it. Tears welled and spilled down her cheeks, and although she was breathing heavily she couldn't get enough air into her burning lungs.

The shards of light faded as her climax waned and she slumped onto Sab with exhaustion. Lethargy crept through her body and she fell into a deep dreamless sleep.

Chapter Eleven

Zara hated that her men were out patrolling the streets in search of the demonic. The only consolation was that they had spent the whole day together. She wanted to be out there with them so she could be assured that they were safe, but she knew she would be more of a liability than a help if she went out with them since she had no real training. But she hated feeling superfluous.

She wandered around the hallways and headed toward Ra's temple. The moment she stepped inside she felt washed in peace. When she made it to the center of the room under the glass pyramid she looked up. Her breath caught in her throat when she saw all the stars glimmering in the sky. She sat down on the floor and closed her eyes.

She'd been meandering through the sentinels' bunker type home for what seemed like hours, not being able to rid herself of the anxiety coursing through her body. She was worried about Set, Sab and the others getting hurt but she tried to push that negativity to the back of her mind. It was difficult for her to be here all alone when they were out trying to keep humanity safe. Zara wanted to be out with them.

With a sigh she stood up and decided to head to the gym she'd found in her wanderings. If she was going to ever be up to par and help her mates fight these shadow demons, she needed to get into shape.

She wasn't fat or unfit but she figured being stronger would be a definite plus if she was ever able to talk her mates around into allowing her out with them.

When she spotted the treadmill she walked up to it and turned it on. She'd never been much of a runner but she had nothing to lose and everything to gain so she stepped onto the machine and started off at a fast walk. Ten minutes later she was sprinting faster than she ever had in her life, which was surprising, but what surprised her even more was that she wasn't even breathless and she should have been. She looked toward the mirror on the far wall that she'd spotted when she first walked into the room and her mouth gaped open. Her arms and legs were moving so fast she was nearly a blur. She suspected that if she didn't have enhanced senses after mating with her two guys, she wouldn't have been able to see herself at all. A smile formed on her face and she decided to see what else she could do.

* * * *

"Shit!" Sab muttered under his breath. "Can any of you get a pinpoint on where the evil is coming from?"

"The demon's in this area, but I can't quite get a fix on the location," Mit said in a quiet yet very angry voice.

"We have to find him before he does too much damage." Set threaded his fingers through his hair. They had been too late to save the young man who'd been walking along the back streets of Price. He hated to lose innocents to those fuckers but what worried him was that the demon had been strong enough to take over a human body. There had been finger marks around the young man's neck and his face had been battered beyond recognition. Set's first instinct had been to pick the body up and bury him since that's what they'd done thousands of years ago, but with the knowledge and technology available to law enforcement and forensic scientists, he was hoping that those humans would find DNA and be able to help lead them to the demon. Although he didn't really think they would.

En was really interested in the law and was often found listening to a scanner. It also allowed them to get information in their searches for the shadow demons. He and the other sentinels were often on a scene before the law and dealt with the demonic before they could steal enough souls to enable them to take over a body.

Any calls that came through the scanner of young frightened men or women were investigated by them, especially after the cops had looked around and reported back to base that they hadn't found anything. Set was glad about the advances humans had made because it made their job a hell of a lot easier.

"To the west," Wen said just before he took off running.

Set and the rest of the sentinels followed their comrade, moving so fast that they couldn't be seen by any humans out and about. It took them approximately a minute, if that, to travel just over ten miles and they were just in time to see the demonic stop a group of young women as they walked along the bank of Gordon Creek.

"Leave us alone." One of the braver women tried to walk around the demon.

"I just want to talk," the demon replied.

"Look, buddy, we just want to be left alone," one of the other women said, shifting nervously on her feet as she glanced about as if looking for an escape route, or someone to help.

All of a sudden the demon lunged forward, grabbing the smallest woman by her wrist and tugging her into his bigger body.

Set drew his sickle shaped sword or scimitar and ran toward the women and demon. Sab and the others followed. When he reached the demon-possessed human, he wrenched the guy away from the woman as Sab, Menna and Pen grabbed the women, lifted them into their arms, and hurried away.

Set released the demon and although the shadow tried to place a hand on his chest to get at his soul, he moved too fast for it to get a hold of him. The body the demon had taken over was sluggish and the skin tone was a sickly pale blue color which reminded him of a dead body. He was just glad the demonic hadn't had the chance to steal enough souls to give it the energy to give him a good fight. If that had been the case Set could have found himself dragged into the underworld before he could blink.

He lifted his sword and with one swing sliced the head from the body. Set watched dispassionately as it fell to the ground, waiting for the shadow to emerge. He didn't have long to wait. Seconds later a dark shadow rose from the dead human and before it had appeared fully he sliced his sword through it.

Eerie shrieks and moans assailed his sensitive ears as the shadow demon writhed in agony and slowly faded to nothing.

"Good job, Set." En squeezed his shoulder.

"Did Sab and the others block the women's memories?" Set asked as he glanced about for the others.

En nodded and was about to reply but no words were necessary when Sab, Pen and Men appeared in front of him.

"The demon didn't hurt that girl?" Set asked.

"Other than a few bruises and scratches on her wrist, no," Sab answered.

"There's something not right about this situation." Set frowned and turned on his heel, heading back toward the town of Price.

"What do you mean?" Paser asked.

"It was too easy."

Wen looked at Set over his shoulder. "It was. The demonic aren't usually so careless until they're at full strength."

"What the hell is Apep up to?" Mit asked with a sigh.

"I think he's building an army," Pen suggested.

"Surely there would have been more activity if he was. People would be reporting their loved ones missing but there's only been one or two here and there." Set reached over, putting his sword back in the sheath strapped to his back.

"No more than usual," En confirmed.

"Then how the hell is Apep going to create his army if the demonic aren't stealing souls from the innocent?" Men asked.

"I don't know, but he's up to something and I don't like it."

* * * *

Zara was having the time of her life. She couldn't believe she could bench press five hundred pounds without straining her muscles. She'd tried every piece of equipment in the gym and did whatever it was with the ease of an elite athlete. No, even better than that. What she really wanted to test was hand to hand fighting.

She was currently standing in front of the large mirror on the wall and going through the moves of some sort of martial arts. There were pictures and descriptions of each move pinned to the wall beside the mirror and she spent the last couple of hours doing each one over and over until they began to feel natural. By the time she was done she was filled with a confidence she'd never had before. Her muscles were pleasantly tired from hours of working out and testing her body, but she wasn't exhausted like she would have been if she hadn't been made immortal, and she wasn't covered in sweat or breathing heavily.

Zara decided she'd had enough for now and sat on the floor so she could cool her body down slowly as she stretched. When she was finished she rose and headed toward the kitchen. She had a feeling the guys would be hungry when they got home and decided to cook them a big breakfast with all the works. Plus, she was thirsty and needed a drink.

After she'd guzzled down a glass of water she set the bacon and eggs on the counter and mixed up a large batch of pancake batter, then set the table. She wasn't sure what time the sentinels would be back and decided to hold off on cooking because she didn't want anything to spoil.

Zara jumped when she heard a bang in the distance and crept into the hallway. She listened intently but when she didn't hear any more noise took a step back toward the kitchen. Another bang came from the vicinity of the entrance and although she was nervous, she wasn't

scared. Set and Sab had told her that no one but them could get into
their home.

She kept moving until she was standing in front of the door and
jumped when another series of bangs hit the steel door. There was a
speaker to one side of the entrance, which Zara activated. She didn't
say anything but listened, hoping whoever was there would speak or
leave, but she couldn't leave some poor soul outside if they were in
trouble.

The entrance to the bunker was disguised as a beach house where
any deliveries were taken. The front room was the only real room in
the house, and no human had ever been beyond that point. The long
hallway at the back off the house led to the underwater bunker, which
had another set of doors that could be closed off if necessary for
safety reasons. Set and Sab added her DNA to the security system
before they left, but she wasn't sure she should open the door.

"Hello?" a female voice whispered. Bang, bang, bang. The
woman's fist hit the door, the sound reverberating down the long
corridor. "Please? Someone help me."

Zara bit her lip in indecision. Set and Sab had told her to stay
inside where she would be safe but she couldn't leave the woman out
there if she was in trouble. She sucked in a breath and then opened the
door.

The woman fell across the threshold and onto the floor. She was
covered in bruises and blood. Zara knelt down and gently turned her
onto her side in case she got sick. She brushed the dark hair from her
face and swore when she saw there was a blue tint to her skin. It
looked like the woman was barely breathing and starting to turn blue.

Zara wondered if she should call 9-1-1 or start CPR on her but
made the choice when the woman's chest stopped rising and falling.
She quickly turned her over onto her back, tipped her head back to
open her airways, pinched her nose, and pulled her chin down to open
her mouth. After checking there was no foreign matter in the

woman's mouth or throat, she covered her mouth with her own and breathed into her.

She knew she'd made a mistake and been had the moment hands clutched hold of her head in a punishing grip. Zara planted her hands on the woman's shoulders and tried to pull back but she seemed to have inhuman strength. A cry of pain emitted from her mouth when sharp fingernails dug into her scalp and although she wrapped her hands around the crazy woman's wrists and tried to pull the woman's hands from her head, she couldn't get her to budge.

Zara jerked when a slimy disgusting tongue slid into her mouth and she gagged as she tried to turn her head to the side. The muscles in her neck wrenched, sending shards of pain shooting into her head and down her spine, but it was the pain in her chest that scared the bejesus out of her.

Zara opened her eyes and stared into the soulless blue ones of the woman she'd tried to help and knew she was in deep shit. What she saw in that gaze made her shake and shiver with fear and she wondered if she would come out of this alive or whole.

Little by little she could feel her spirit being drawn from her body and darkness began to close in.

The image of Set and Sab popped into her head, their eyes had been so full of love when they'd made love to her and her heart stuttered before slamming against the wall of her chest. Anger began to build. She'd only just found men who loved her unconditionally and she loved them so much in return, she didn't want to die or be the underworld demon ruler's puppet.

Zara let the adrenaline flow through her blood and compounded her anger until she felt as if she was in a full blown rage. She wasn't giving up without a fight. If she was going out then it would be in a blaze of glory.

* * * *

Sab stumbled and almost went to his knees when he felt agony pierce his chest. A roar of fury and fear left his mouth and he turned to look at Set. His friend had a hand on his chest and his face had gone pale.

"Zara!" Set shouted and then took off.

The speed Sab and Set ran at was exceptionally fast. Faster than they'd ever pushed themselves before. They had to travel approximately seventy five miles to get back to the base and although they'd come by van, they didn't have time to go back to the vehicle. Not with Zara in danger and when it was faster to travel this way by foot.

"Teleport!" Set ordered, hoping like hell he and Sab wouldn't be too disorientated to be able to save their mate. He cursed when they came up short and began to run again. He and the others were going to have to start using this skill more often so they could become more proficient at it. Hopefully the effects of teleporting would lesson.

"What's going on?" Pen asked as he and the others caught up with Sab and Set.

"I think this was a set-up, meant to keep us busy while one of the demonic got to our woman."

"Fuck!" Mit nodded and the team of sentinels ran like they'd never run before.

Sab prayed to Ra and any other god willing to listen to keep Zara safe. He knew without a shadow of a doubt that if he lost her now, after just finding her, he wouldn't be able to go on. She had become his world and he would do absolutely anything to save her.

Even give his own life.

* * * *

Zara could feel her spirit slowing draining away, but she didn't stop fighting. She embraced the anger racing through her body but she also tried to keep her mind in the game. She moved her hands to the woman's throat and squeezed so hard she felt the woman's trachea and esophagus give way.

She managed to get a knee to the floor and pushed her body up and off the possessed woman's, shifted her other knee and pressed it against her chest. The demon inside the female roared with pain and anger but Zara held her ground as much as she could, using all of her newfound strength. When the woman's eyes rolled back in her head and her hands fell away from Zara's hair and head to flop to the floor, she eased her hold on her throat, but wasn't stupid enough to leave her unrestrained.

Now that she felt the danger had passed her body began to react. Her frame began to tremble and tears welled in her eyes and although she wished Set and Sab were here to hold her, she was still all alone. She didn't even realize she was hyperventilating until dark spots formed before her eyes, but when she did she held her breath for a few moments before exhaling slowly. The darkness receded but she was still shaking and her teeth were chattering. Cold had permeated her frame to the bone and all she wanted to do was have a hot shower and curl up in bed, but first she had to find a way to tie this crazy bitch up.

Zara slowly and carefully removed her knee from the female's chest, watching her intently just in case she was playing at being unconscious. When she remained still on the floor, Zara sighed with relief and rose to her feet, before hurrying toward the kitchen. She needed to find something to use to restrain the woman and hope that the bitch didn't escape the bindings and come at her again before her mates and the other sentinels got back.

She rummaged through cupboards and when she didn't find anything she searched the drawers. She nearly shouted in triumph when she found a bunch of zip ties. Zara grabbed them and a knife for protection just in case and headed back to the prone demon-possessed woman.

The moment she was close enough to see the floor near the entrance Zara froze and then she glanced about, fear spiking in her body again. The demonic bitch was gone but Zara had a feeling she hadn't gone far. Even though the lights were on there were too many shadows for her to see clearly and too many places to hide. There were numerous doors off of the hallway and all of them were closed. Zara didn't want to risk going into one of those rooms only to be jumped and end up demon fodder. She decided that maybe she would have a better chance of surviving this by going outside. At least she would have more places to run to and hopefully she'd be able to find a hiding place. She didn't think a locked door would be much of a deterrent to the demon, especially since Zara had had a taste of the fucker's strength.

Keeping alert with the knife gripped tightly in her right hand and the zip ties in her left, Zara backed toward the open door and kept her glance moving, watching for a glimpse of the demon or movement in the shadows.

She'd just stepped over the threshold and outside when she felt a frission of cold race up her spine. The hair on the back of her neck stood on end and she slowly turned to face the threat. What she saw in front of her had her mouth gaping open in terror and her knees trembled so much she didn't think she would be able to remain standing for much longer.

There were about ten wispy-like shadows floating in the air and then as one they surrounded her. She glanced to her right when she saw movement and saw the demon-possessed bitch moving toward her. When the woman moved her arm, and Zara saw the evil bitch had a knife, she gulped. She hadn't even realized she'd dropped the knife as she'd frozen in terror.

* * * *

Set's legs were burning from moving so fast for so long. What should have taken them just over an hour to travel, took them just less than a quarter of that time, thanks to teleporting some of the way. He'd never been so scared in his life than when he'd felt that god-awful excruciating pain in his chest, and it hadn't been the pain that had scared him. It was where the source of pain was coming from.

The moment he saw the copse of trees and then the beach house on the edge of the lake, hiding the entrance to the compound, he and Sab slowed down. He needed to use his head and not go off half-cocked, which could put Zara in more danger or end up getting her killed.

He moved up behind the last tree before the clearing and his heart stopped. She was surrounded by shadow demons, and a demon-possessed human was walking slowly toward her with a knife in her hand. He wished he could call on Ra, but the sun god had never manifested at night time. It was up to him, Sab, and the other sentinels to save his mate. Thankfully, there was something wrong with the human's body because it was moving as if in slow motion.

Set gave the others hand signals and waited until they were in position. He glanced at Sab and saw the same look of determination on his friend's face that was probably on his. With a nod, he reached back, withdrew his sword, and walked toward his mate.

Half the shadow demonic broke off from the group and floated toward him and Sab. Set stopped and loosened his muscles in preparation of the fight to come. The first demon to get close to him opened its mouth, emitting a high pitched eerie cry which hurt his ears, but he blocked it as best he could. When he saw the other demonic move toward his mate he roared with rage. Sab's war cry joined his and they began slashing through the shadows while the rest of the sentinels hurried toward Zara.

He and Sab swung without cessation and before he knew it the shadows who'd turned to fight them were no longer. The other sentinels had surrounded the other demons but none of them had taken the chance to slash at them.

Those fucking demonic had encased their mate in their shadows and if any of them tried to kill them they would end up hurting and maybe even killing Zara. They couldn't take the chance. Her body was weeping blood from cuts where the demonic had been holding her.

The instant his gaze locked with Zara's and he saw the terror in her eyes, his anger erupted until he began to shake with rage.

"Take me and let her go," Set stepped toward the shadows and Zara, praying the demonic would take him up on his offer so his mate would be safe.

"Set, no!" Zara yelled.

"I can't let them have you, baby." Set pushed all the love he felt for his mate into the link between them and toward her.

Her eyes softened and she stared at him and then Sab with her heart in her eyes. The love that shone from her gaze was so pure and true it made his heart hurt.

Just as the possessed human grabbed hold of Zara's hair, tugging her head back at an unnatural angle, and placed the knife blade to his mate's throat, Set began to move.

And then the most amazing thing happened.

The glow of love in Zara's eyes seemed to shine out and started to flow over her body until she was covered in pure white light.

The shadow demons screamed. As if silently screaming, the possessed human's mouth gaped open. Then there was a loud explosion. The demon-possessed woman and the shadow demons disintegrated into ashes. Although the light had burst up and out and covered him and the other sentinels, Set was amazed that none of them were harmed. The light faded and he had to blink a few times to adjust to the darkness. When he was able to see, his heart stopped for a second and then he was on the move.

Set threw himself to his knees, aware of Sab doing the same and he reached for Zara. She was prone on the ground and even though she wasn't conscious he was relieved to see that she was breathing. He tore open one of the rips in her shirt and was amazed to see the cuts which had been on her body were gone. Her skin was unmarred, except for the drying blood. No scars had been left to blemish her perfect skin.

"Man, that was fucking awesome," Wen whispered in an awe filled voice.

"Is she all right?" Pen asked as he came up behind Sab.

"I'm not sure." Set lifted Zara into his arms and then stood. "We need to get her back inside."

"Do you want me to call Ra?" En asked.

"I don't know if he can come to us during the dark hours. He never has before. Perhaps you could check her out first." Set hurried inside and didn't stop until he was in the rooms he shared with Sab.

Sab hurried to the bed, pulled the covers back and Set gently lowered Zara to the mattress. He and Sab removed her shoes and then waited anxiously while En looked their mate over.

When En was done he turned to face Set and Sab. "She seems fine. Her heart rate and breathing are normal. Maybe that burst of power took everything out of her. I suggest you let her sleep and if she doesn't wake up after a few hours, we'll call Ra in."

Set nodded and began to pace as the other sentinels left.

"Did you feel it?" Sab asked.

Set nodded. "I've never felt anything so…"

"Yeah," Sab sighed and scrubbed a hand over his face.

"Do you think she'll be okay?" Set asked.

"Only time will tell, friend. Only time will tell."

Set knew Sab was right but what worried him was that he couldn't feel Zara through their mating connection at all now. He wished he and Sab hadn't left her alone tonight. If they had stayed with her none of this would have ever happened.

Hindsight was a wonderful thing, but he couldn't change the past, much to his disgust.

Set knew he wasn't going to sleep a wink. There wasn't a chance in hell he was closing his eyes until Zara opened hers and he knew she was going to be all right.

Chapter Twelve

Zara bolted upright and gasped. Her heart pounded and she panted, her gaze skittering around as she searched for her mates. As soon as she saw them both lying in bed on either side of her she sighed with relief.

All of a sudden Set rolled from the bed, bounded to his feet and looked about the room as if for a threat.

"There's no one here," Zara said quietly, hoping to reassure him.

"Zara! You're awake." Set crawled onto the bed and pulled her into his arms.

Zara breathed in his delectable manly scent and relished having his bare chest against her cheek.

Sab moved into her until his front was pressed against her back and wrapped an arm around her waist. "We were so worried about you." He kissed her shoulder. "Why the hell did you open the fucking door?"

Zara rolled over onto her back so that she could see both of her mates. She'd never heard that tone from Sab before, especially when he was talking to her, but since the bond between them seemed to be at full strength she understood it. He'd been scared and worried sick for her.

"I'm sorry. I know I shouldn't have opened the door but I didn't know that woman had been possessed by a demonic." Zara went on to explain the situation to when they'd found her surrounded by the shadow demons.

"You scared ten years off my life," Set said in a growly voice.

"Since you're immortal I don't think that makes a difference."

"Smartass," Sab said and although he tried to keep the smile from his face he wasn't successful.

Zara chuckled and was pleased when Set and Sab did, too. Their laughter was cathartic after the previous night's events. The more she laughed the more light hearted she felt. That was until Set rested his palm on her stomach and pressed his lips to hers. She was about to kiss him back but he pulled away before she could initiate anything.

"Do you remember what happened to the shadow demons?" Sab asked and she could hear the curiosity in his voice, but that wasn't all, he sounded sort of smug.

"Um, sort of."

"You killed them all," Set said. "But I'm not sure how."

Zara's cheeks heated but she took a deep breath, reached out and clasped one each of their hands and said, "It's because I love you both so much. I couldn't stand the thought of you taking my place and being hurt. When I looked into each of your gazes I could see so much emotion there and I couldn't let Set trade places with me.

"The most amazing calm, peaceful feeling washed over me as I made my decision to sacrifice myself and my heart and soul filled with so much love. I don't know how it was possible but I think my love for you two was strong enough to kill those demons."

"God, honey, you are so fucking amazing." Sab brought her hand to his mouth and kissed the back of it. "I didn't realize how empty my life was until I met you. I love you more than anything in this entire world. You're so special."

Zara swallowed around the tight constriction in her throat but she couldn't stop the tears burning her eyes from forming or spilling down her cheeks.

Set squeezed her hand, drawing her attention. "I love you, Zara Barry. You are every breath I take and I never want to be without you."

A sob of happiness erupted from Zara's mouth and she got to her knees and turned around the face her men who were both leaning against the headboard. "Thank you for such a wonderful gift. I never thought I would find one man to love me that way, let alone two. I feel like I've been blessed by the gods."

"Maybe we all have been."

"What do you mean?" Zara asked Sab.

"Ra told us that he would reward us for our thousands of years of loyalty and servitude. He sent us to you."

Zara nodded and then lifted her head toward the ceiling. "Thank you, Ra."

"You're welcome child," Ra replied in a loud booming voice which made her startle and she shivered when the power of his presence washed over her before it waned again.

"Do you think you could train me to fight the demonic?" Zara asked and then waited with bated breath for a reply.

"Yeah," Set sighed. "After tonight you need to know how to defend yourself against the shadow demons. Although I think you have more power than all of us combined with that light thing you have happening, but I would feel a hell of a lot better knowing you could wield a sword and take those fuckers down."

"Good." Zara smiled. "When can we start training?"

"Tomorrow," Sab replied as he slid down the bed then tugged her on top of him.

Zara shrieked with surprise and then laughed. Her laughter was cut short when Sab cupped her cheeks in his hands and drew her mouth to his.

She opened to him when his tongue swept over her lips and then moaned as he delved inside. He tasted so good, so right and she knew she was home. Sab kissed her deeply, wildly, passionately and her body responded with desire. Her wet pussy clenched, begging to be filled and her clit throbbed right along with her heartbeat.

She whimpered with frustration when Sab broke the kiss but nearly cheered him and Set on when they stood and shucked their boxer shorts. Zara was so famished for her men she quickly whipped the sleeping shirt she had on up and over her head before she pushed her panties down her legs and kicked them away.

Set dove on the bed right between her legs and before she could take another breath he pushed her thighs further apart and covered her cunt with his mouth. She moaned as he licked through her folds and bucked her hips up trying to get his tongue on her needy clit, but it seemed he had other plans.

Set flipped her over, pulled her to her hands and knees and it was only then she noticed that Sab had gotten onto the bed. He was reclining with a pillow at his back and against the headboard. His legs were splayed and his long thick cock was bobbing gently along with his heartbeat.

Saliva pooled in Zara's mouth and she crawled forward until she was between his spread thighs. She gripped the base of his cock, pumped her hand up and down his erection a few times and then she bent over and twirled her tongue over the head of his hard dick.

He groaned and when she sucked the head of his rod into her mouth his hand moved to her nape and he gripped her hair. "So fucking good, honey. Your mouth is so hot and wet. Suck me, Zara. Make me come in your mouth."

Zara hummed and then began to bob her head up and down, taking him a little deeper each time. She moaned around his cock when Set caressed her clit and dipped a finger into her cunt. She wiggled her ass at him, begging him without words to fill her pussy with his cock.

When she felt Set's thighs against her ass and her own, she spread her legs more and sighed as he began to breach her. Their bond was open and the love they felt for each other was flowing back and forth and her heart was so full of joy she felt like it might just burst.

She groaned when Set gripped her hips and then cried out with pleasure as he surged into her wet pussy balls-deep. Zara took as much of Sab's cock in as she could and when he touched the back of her throat she inhaled through her nose and relaxed her muscles.

"Fuck yeah. That's it, honey. Swallow around me," Sab said between panting breaths.

Zara cupped his balls in her hand and gently rolled them as she slid her mouth up and down over his cock. His groans and moans mixed with her muffled ones as Set pounded into her hard and fast.

The tension built quickly and Zara knew it wouldn't be long before she reached her peak but she wanted her mates to come with her. She pushed down onto Sab's cock as she carefully squeezed his testicles and she flexed her cunt muscles.

Set made a growly noise and then he increased the speed of his gliding cock. Molten heat spread out from her womb and encompassed her whole body. She pushed her love out toward her men and cried out as she hovered on the precipice.

When she felt Sab's testes harden and draw up closer to his body and his cock begin to pulse she knew he was about to lose his load. Zara swallowed again and then her, Sab's and Set's cries of release echoed around the room.

Zara gulped down Sab's cum and tried to stay up on her hands and knees as her cunt clamped around Set's jerking dick before releasing only to contract around him again.

It was one of the most powerful and profound climaxes of her life. Her whole life had changed for the better and she was so happy to have found her two mates.

She'd never really believed in God or any deity but she'd always thought that there had to be some truth to the stories of the heavens. Now she knew that the sun god, Ra existed, she had a feeling there were a lot more deities in the heavens watching over humanity. Peace was something humans had being trying to achieve for thousands of years and now that the gods were on their side and she had two demigods at hers, maybe good would win over evil after all.

However what she looked forward to the most was spending as much time as she could with her mates and showing them how much she loved them.

Zara felt as if she had been truly blessed for the first time in her life and she was going to give thanks each and every day.

THE END

WWW.BECCAVAN-EROTICROMANCE.COM

ABOUT THE AUTHOR

My name is Becca Van. I live in Australia with my wonderful hubby of many years, as well as my two children.

I read my first romance, which I found in the school library, at the age of thirteen and haven't stopped reading them since. It is so wonderful to know that love is still alive and strong when there seems to be so much conflict in the world.

I dreamed of writing my own book one day but, unfortunately, didn't follow my dream for many years. But once I started, I knew writing was what I wanted to continue doing.

I love to escape from the world and curl up with a good romance, to see how the characters unfold and conflict is dealt with. I have read many books and love all facets of the romance genre, from historical to erotic romance. I am a sucker for a happy ending.

For all titles by Becca Van, please visit
www.bookstrand.com/becca-van

Siren Publishing, Inc.
www.SirenPublishing.com

Lightning Source UK Ltd.
Milton Keynes UK
UKOW06f0618170816

280869UK00016B/366/P